Summer gaze
"Are you coming in, or what?"

Beau smiled down at her. He unbuckled his belt and dropped his Levi's. He yanked off his baseball cap and tossed it next to his T-shirt.

She grinned. "Will you just jump already?"

And then he did. He hit the water next to her, making as much of a splash as possible. It was so cold, it felt like his heart might stop as he kicked his way to the surface. When he broke it, he gasped.

She laughed again as he shook his hair, spraying her with water.

He moved closer, and his legs brushed hers. Even with the goose bumps along her skin, she felt impossibly soft underneath the water.

His gaze locked with hers, water dripping into his eyes, blurring them.

She reached up and ran her thumb along his eyebrow. "You're awfully cute, Beau Evers."

"And you're beautiful."

She could probably tell he was getting ready to kiss her. Honestly, he didn't know how he'd waited this long. He'd been afraid of so many things. But mostly, he'd been afraid of falling for her again.

But he realized, as his lips met hers, that it was too damn late.

He'd already fallen.

Dear Reader,

Can I just say this is my favorite part? Being able to write you a letter, getting to feel close to you while you hold this book (hopefully somewhere comfy!) as you get ready to step inside another Christmas Bay story in the Hearts on Main Street miniseries. This one, Beau and Summer's, was *so* fun to write. Like Beau, my husband is also a fisherman—a lover of all things river—so it was near and dear to my Oregonian heart.

Thank you for being here, for holding this book, for taking this journey with me. I hope this little town on the coast feels as real to you as it does to me and that you'll want to shake your beach blanket off, pull your sunglasses out and stay awhile.

Happy reading!

Kaylie Newell

HIS SMALL-TOWN CATCH

KAYLIE NEWELL

Recycling programs for this product may not exist in your area.

ISBN-13: 978-1-335-40227-1

His Small-Town Catch

For questions and comments about the quality of this book, please contact us at CustomerService@Harlequin.com.

TM and ® are trademarks of Harlequin Enterprises ULC.

Harlequin Enterprises ULC
22 Adelaide St. West, 41st Floor
Toronto, Ontario M5H 4E3, Canada
www.Harlequin.com

Printed in U.S.A.

For **Kaylie Newell**, storytelling is in the blood. Growing up the daughter of two writers, she knew eventually she'd want to follow in their footsteps. She's now the proud author of over twenty books, including the RITA® Award finalists *Christmas at the Graff* and *Tanner's Promise*.

Kaylie lives in Southern Oregon with her husband, two daughters, a blind Doberman and two indifferent cats. Visit Kaylie at Facebook.com/kaylienewell.

Books by Kaylie Newell

Montana Mavericks: The Anniversary Gift

The Maverick's Marriage Deal

Harlequin Special Edition

Hearts on Main Street

Flirting with the Past
His Small-Town Catch

Sisters of Christmas Bay

Their Sweet Coastal Reunion
Their All-Star Summer
Their Christmas Resolution

Visit the Author Profile page
at Harlequin.com for more titles.

For Matt—my favorite fisherman.

Chapter One

Beau Evers would rather be fishing.

That's the thought that kept reverberating through his head as he stood behind the counter of his grandfather's antique shop on Christmas Bay's historic Main Street.

He watched the tourists walking by outside the old single-paned windows—coffees in their hands, bags slung over their shoulders, the summer sun shining brightly overhead—and wondered for the thousandth time how he'd ended up here at thirty. This wasn't how his life was supposed to be unfolding.

Shifting on his feet, he ground his teeth together. He was too serious. That's what his cousins called him. Also a grump. That's what his niece called him. But he had a good reason for being both since fishing was basically off the table until he got his shoulder surgery, which wasn't scheduled for another month. He'd managed to get in with a rock star orthopedic surgeon in Portland, some lady who'd just operated on a pitcher for the Mariners, but she had a waiting list a mile long.

Taking a sip of coffee, he scalded his tongue.

"Crap," he muttered and set the mug down again, coffee sloshing over the side and onto his hand. Grabbing a dishtowel from under the counter, he looked over at an elderly lady perusing the kitchen items and felt his chest tighten. No, he definitely wasn't supposed to be running an antique shop of all things. Especially not with his formerly estranged cousins, Poppy and Cora Sawyer, but their grandfather Earl had passed away a few months ago and had left the shop to them. Well, temporarily. His will had stipulated that they needed to run it together for a year in order to get their inheritance. Only at the end of that year could they sell—if they wanted to.

It was a brilliant move by a man whose dying wish had been to see his family reunited by any means necessary. They had to hand it to him. He'd usually gotten what he'd wanted. The truth was Beau and his cousins had loved Earl very much and none of them cared about the inheritance. But it was also true that they all *needed* their inheritance, and their grandfather had known that.

So Beau leaned against the counter and tried again to push away that ever-present thought of *I'd rather be fishing* and concentrate on the fact that he was going to be running this shop for a while now and the less he ruminated on that the better. What was it Cora said? Live in the moment? He'd try. Even if he couldn't help but wonder what the fish were biting on this very minute.

"This teapot is cracked," the elderly woman said from a few aisles away. She held the offending pot above her gray head triumphantly. "Would you take less for it?"

Beau stifled a groan. He didn't like haggling with people. Poppy was better at that than he was. He was the furniture guy, the one who bought the bigger inventory. That meant he usually got to work from the office in back and didn't have to deal with the customers at all, which was just the way he liked it. But this was Saturday and on Saturdays Cora and Poppy had a standing girls' date with Mary, his eleven-year-old niece. They all went out to lunch and got their nails done afterward. Or their toes. Or whatever needed doing at that particular point in time. Cora had lost her husband to cancer not long before their grandfather had passed, so her daughter was having a hard time acclimating to life in a new town, as well as grieving the loss of her stepfather who'd raised her since she was a baby.

Beau smiled. "Let me take a quick look and I'll see what I can do."

The elderly woman pursed her lips, obviously hoping he'd just give her the discount already. And maybe he should've. He had no idea what he was doing.

The door to the shop opened with a tinkle of the little bell above it and Beau looked up with his standard greeting on his tongue. But when he saw the woman who'd walked inside, her long red hair pulled into a loose side braid, he found he couldn't speak at all.

"It's a big crack," the elderly woman called over again. She hadn't moved an inch. She was apparently going to hold her ground, dead set on getting that discount before making her way over to Beau and the vintage cash register. Maybe she had enough superglue at home to render cracks meaningless.

"Uh..." Beau forced his gaze away from the redhead who'd taken off her sunglasses and was now looking around the shop with interest. "How about twenty-five percent off?" He had no idea if that's how much his grandfather would've taken off, but it seemed fair enough. Plus, he was having a hard time engaging at all.

Teapots were not the number-one thing on his mind at the moment.

The elderly woman's bright pink lips eased into a smile. She seemed happy with that.

He glanced at the redhead again but made sure she didn't see him glancing. It couldn't be. Could it? After all these years? What would she be doing in Christmas Bay? He considered this even as another thought bounced across his consciousness. *Her family was from Eugene. That's not that far away from the coast and a ton of people come over here in the summers...*

He was sure he could smell her perfume, but that was ridiculous because she was all the way across the shop. It was the memory of her perfume that was messing with his head. That was threatening to knock the wind right out of him.

Narrowing his eyes, he watched her walk over to an antique coffee table and run her fingers lightly over the top. She seemed lost in her own little world. A world of things from long ago, of lives from long ago. Which was fitting, actually. He was lost in the past right then, too.

The elderly woman shuffled up to the counter, clutching the teapot with both hands. She looked proud of her find. Even prouder of the fact that she was getting it for a discount. She smiled at Beau and soft wrinkles exploded from the corners of her eyes. He felt instantly guilty at being annoyed with her haggling. Was that even what she'd been doing? He wasn't sure if it qualified. His grandpa would've known. Would probably have had her eating out of his hand by now.

"I just love this shop," she said, sliding the teapot across the counter. "I try to come in whenever I'm in town."

"Oh?" Beau rang her up then reached for the tissue paper underneath the counter. The redhead was now bending over to look more closely at the coffee table, and again he had to keep himself from staring. "Where are you from?"

"Springfield originally. But when my husband died, I moved into a retirement community in Eugene. It's closer to my kids."

Eugene. Another reminder that Christmas Bay was close. Close enough for an afternoon drive. Close enough for someone from his past to show up here.

"I used to live in Eugene," he said. "Go Ducks."

"Well, my granddaughter goes to Oregon State, so I have to say 'Go Beavers.'"

"Ah."

"Where's the man who usually works here? Older, white hair?" She smiled. "I haven't seen him in a while. He looks like an older Paul Newman with those sparkling eyes."

Beau's throat constricted. The loss of his grandpa was still so fresh that he sometimes forgot. And then something would jolt him back to reality—a well-meaning question, a memory, a scent. And the grief would come crashing back again. "That was my grandfather," he said. "He passed this spring."

"Oh no." Her expression fell. "I'm sorry to hear that, honey. My condolences. He was always so nice, so helpful."

"Yes, he was."

"So you're running the shop now? How wonderful."

Beau had gotten this a few times. The truth was he wouldn't be for long. But he'd found it was easier not to go into the details. *My cousins and I are, but only until next year. I'm a fisherman and I have to get back on the water, yada, yada, yada.* The more information he gave people, the unhappier they were. They wanted to know the shop would continue on as it always had—especially the regular tourists who kept coming back again and again, season after season, year after year.

So he kept his mouth shut now and smiled as he handed over the teapot, all wrapped up and packed in a trendy, shabby-chic shopping bag that had Earl's Antiques embossed in gold foil on the front. Cora had ordered them a few weeks ago. She said everyone liked a nice bag to take their things home in. He didn't know about that, but they'd been expensive enough. Maybe people just liked to feel like they'd splurged and had gotten something extra in the process.

"Thank you, hon," she said. "Have a good day."

"You have a good one, too. And drive safe."

She turned and shuffled toward the door, her bag hooked over one arm. Beau watched her put on a pair of dark sunglasses that looked more like goggles and push the door open into the bright coastal morning. No sun was getting past those suckers.

And then the shop was empty again. Except for the redhead, of course.

He looked over to where she was inspecting an antique vanity. It had been so long since he'd seen Summer Smith, almost a dozen years to be exact, that he really wasn't sure if it was her or not. He still hadn't gotten a good look at her face. But it was the way she moved, gracefully and with gentle intention, that was making his shoulders stiffen now. He remembered how soft her body had been, how sexy her voice had sounded when she'd said his name. And that had been how it was for an entire year. The best year of his life, if he was honest. But he'd had all kinds of commitment issues, and he'd been selfish and arrogant and young, and he'd quit college to fish full-time because that was his dream and he hadn't wanted any distractions. He'd said goodbye to her one autumn day when the leaves had fallen like rust-colored rain all around them. She'd cried. He hadn't.

He'd thought about her a lot over the years. About things he wished he'd done differently. Things he wished he hadn't. But he'd never thought about tracking her down. He hadn't even looked her up on social media. Mary called it "stalking the socials." Apparently that kind of stalking was perfectly acceptable when you were in middle school. And maybe it was when you were thirty, too. He didn't really know. The only social media he ever bothered with was his official fishing page, and he barely used that.

She turned and fixed him with a smile. "This is gorgeous," she said. "How much—" And then that smile he remembered so well wilted on her lips. The color drained from her face, though she already had a pale complexion. Freckles were scattered across her nose and the apples of her cheeks, freckles that he remembered she'd hated. He'd loved them. One night he'd kissed those freckles slowly and tenderly until he'd come to the feathery softness of her lips. He'd never been good at telling her how he'd felt. But he'd been pretty good at showing it.

The blood rushed in his ears now. Only it wasn't rushing. It was pounding. Like rapids in the river, the water beating violently over the slick blackness of the rocks.

"Beau?"

Her voice sounded different. Of course, it would. She'd matured, that was obvious in the way the skin had softened around her eyes, around her mouth. But she was still beautiful. Actually, she was even more beautiful now, and that was saying something. She'd been a sight to behold at nineteen.

"Summer," he managed.

They stood there for a minute just looking at each other. Beau said a silent prayer that nobody else would come into the shop. Or maybe he wished someone would. The thickness in the air was almost unbearable.

She stepped toward him. Her eyes were just as green as before. Just as clear.

"What are you doing here?" she asked. "You live in Christmas Bay?"

"Kind of. I'm running the shop with my cousins for a while."

She looked around, her eyes widening. She'd known his family was from Christmas Bay. That his grandfather had a shop there. But that was over a decade ago. She'd obviously forgotten the details.

"I thought you'd still be in Eugene," she said. "Or, actually, I wasn't sure where you'd be now... Are you still fishing?"

If she felt any lingering bitterness about how things had ended between them, she didn't show it. Sport fishing had always been the other woman in their relationship. One that Summer had tried standing up to, but had never been able to compete with in the end. That other woman had been too sexy, too tempting, too romantic. She had lured Beau away with nothing more than the whisper of a promise of a successful future doing what he loved, and that was all it had taken.

"I am," he said. "Sponsored now." *At least for the time being*, he thought uneasily. His sponsor wasn't going to wait forever.

She nodded. "So you're fishing in those big tournaments? The ones you were always interested in?"

He not only fished them, he usually won them. He didn't like to brag, but it was a fact. He'd made a pretty good living turning pro. Until his shoulder had taken a dump on him, that is.

"I've got an injury that needs surgery," he said, "so I'm taking a break until I can get that done. But I'm hoping to get back to it soon."

She frowned. "Your bad shoulder?"

He actually had two bad shoulders now. The first injury he'd gotten playing football in high school. The scar tissue was so extensive in that one that he'd taught himself to cast with his right arm. Later, it was Summer who'd encouraged him to perfect that casting arm and make it not just functional but golden. She'd been nothing but loving and supportive, and look how he'd repaid her. By leaving her. By breaking her heart.

He knew she'd taken it hard; they'd had mutual friends who never missed a chance to tell him how she was. But on the one occasion he'd seen her in town, she'd looked stoic, barely glancing in his direction before walking away. He'd had to stop himself from going after her out of sheer habit. Their relationship had consisted mostly of him messing up and then trying to fix it but failing miserably. Until he'd just gotten tired of trying to be what she needed, which was a stable, loving presence in her life. He really was an ass.

She stood there now, watching him with an expression that was hard to read. It wasn't quite warm but it wasn't quite cold, either. It was indifferent, maybe, and that cut even now. Even after all these years.

"It's my other shoulder," he said. "I fell on a rock. Stupid."

"Oh… I'm sorry."

"It's fine."

She nodded. At one point, she'd known him better than anyone. She'd known when he was feeding her a line. Did she know that now? Did she care? Probably not.

"Well," she said. "I guess I should tell you why I'm here."

"Not just shopping?"

"No, I actually restore and sell antique furniture."

Beau's gaze dropped to her throat where a small diamond necklace sparkled. It looked like the necklace that he'd given her for her twentieth birthday. She'd loved her birthday, had loved all the milestone holidays, so he'd known he needed to go all-out.

Her pulse tapped delicately above the stone, a place that he imagined would be warm and soft. Smelling like her perfume. He told himself that her showing up like this was just a coincidence. He didn't believe in fate. Not very romantic, but it was what it was.

"Oh yeah?" he said.

"Do you work with dealers?"

"I do."

"And private parties?"

"We work with private parties, too."

She licked her lips, which had always been one of her best features in Beau's opinion.

"I know we have a history," she said. "I hope this isn't awkward. But would you be interested in working together? I'm trying to get my business up and running, and your shop has a great reputation. I could show you a few pieces that I have in my truck, so you can get an idea of what my work looks like?"

Beau grit his teeth, feeling that same old hesitation creep in. As much as he'd loved Summer, and he *had* loved her, he didn't want to feel like he owed her anything. He didn't want to be tied to her through guilt or friendship, or anything else. He knew his past had a lot to do with that—his parents' divorce in high school, and Poppy's car accident, where her boyfriend had been killed. Those things had changed Beau fundamentally in his teenage years—changed how he approached relationships of any kind. You didn't want to get close to people because they might leave. Or worse, they might die. And you didn't want them to get close to you because that's where expectations crept in and those never ended well.

This was why fishing suited him so perfectly. It was a solitary job, and Beau had always been a loner at heart.

But he wasn't fishing. He was working in an antique shop where relationships like this were their bread and butter. He was learning there was a fair amount of schmoozing in this business, something he was lousy at. So…what choice did he really have?

Summer stood there watching him. He didn't think he was imagining the slight tilt to her chin. The one that said, *I'm not going to let you intimidate me with that surly attitude, mister.* He could almost hear her saying something like that years ago. She'd been the only one who'd gotten through his walls. Which, of course, was why he'd had to walk away. Actually, he'd practically run away, but whatever.

He stuck his hands in his jeans' pockets. "Sure," he said. "Let's take a look."

She turned and headed for the door. Following her, his gaze dropped to her shapely rear end and his mouth went dry. She was curvier than she'd been before. It looked good on her. She was soft and voluptuous. Beau had never really had a type, but if he had, it would've been just… Summer. She was one of those women who was beautiful no matter what. Probably because she was so beautiful on the inside, a fact that had never escaped him. Even when he'd been busy heading in the opposite direction.

Stepping ahead of her, he opened the door. She walked past, smelling like some kind of fruity shampoo. She gave him a quick look but he couldn't read it. Did she feel weird about this? Was she still mad about how things had ended between them? He wouldn't have blamed her if she was. Whatever she was feeling, though, it was clear she was going to ignore it because she was here for one thing and one thing only. Business.

She walked over to a faded blue Ford, probably only a few years shy of being a classic, and pointed to a pair of end tables strapped together in the bed.

"Mid-century modern," she said with an unmistakable look of pride. "My specialty. I sanded them down and refinished them. Tightened up the legs, they were a little wobbly. Otherwise, they're in great shape."

Beau leaned over the bed of the truck to take a closer

look. He didn't have the natural eye for furniture like Cora did, but he was getting better at it. He and his cousins had worked in the antique shop after school and over summer vacations growing up, and their grandfather had taught them well. He could immediately tell she'd done a good job. These were pieces that usually went like hotcakes in the shop. People couldn't get enough of them.

"Nice," he said, leaning back again. "Really nice work, Summer. I could sell those."

"Yeah?"

The sun beat down on the back of his neck, warming him all over. Or maybe that was Summer. Lovely Summer, whose memory still danced behind his eyes despite his trying to will it away. He remembered Poppy asking him what in the world he'd been thinking after he'd broken up with Summer. He hadn't been able to give her a good answer. At least not one that had made any sense.

"Yeah," he said. "You're talented."

She smiled. "Thanks. It's taken me a while to get to this point."

"It's a definite skill."

"It is, but I wasn't talking about the furniture."

He watched her.

After a few seconds, she crossed her arms over her chest. "I just mean life. You know. Life in general."

"How have you been, Summer?" The question came so easily that it surprised him. Maybe not the words so much as the tone of his voice. It was quiet. Tender almost.

"I've been pretty good. After graduation I had an office job, but I wasn't happy there. I think I was just unhappy in general."

There was an awkward beat or two where he wondered if she was talking about him. Or their breakup. But before he could fall any farther down that wormhole, she shrugged.

"I kept thinking what it would be like to start my own business," she said. "To quit and restore furniture full-time. So I saved for a while to build up some cushion, and now here I am. It's a little scary, but we have to follow our dreams, right?"

Now he was sure she was talking about him. Fishing had been his dream.

"How's your family?" he asked.

"Oh, you know. The same. Mom and Dad retired last year and are in Arizona, they travel a lot. My sister and her husband just had a baby. She lives in Washington now."

"You two were so close. I'm surprised."

"I didn't want to leave Oregon," she said. "And my best friend Angie lives nearby. We see each other all the time, so I still feel like there's family here."

"Are you still in Eugene?"

"Actually, I live right outside of Christmas Bay. I had a little…thing with a coworker, and I wanted to move somewhere quiet."

A thing. He nodded slowly, wondering who this guy was. And then wondering why he was wondering. The most important bit he could take away from her last sentence was that she lived here. Which meant he was probably going to be seeing her again. Even if he wasn't thinking about buying her pieces on a regular basis, which he was.

"I have a little house on an acre," she continued. "Big enough for a shop. And I have a goat. His name is Tank."

He felt the corners of his mouth tug into a smile. She'd always been an animal lover. He remembered a calendar hanging in her dorm room of baby goats in sweaters. He'd teased her about it.

"So you finally got your goat," he said.

"I got my goat."

"And his name is Tank."

"Well, I wanted a Pygmy goat, you probably remember that, but Tank was being rehomed by the county. He'd been neglected and was in pretty bad shape, just skin and bones, so I brought him home. He's huge. And acts like a dog. Follows me everywhere."

Imagining gorgeous, elegant Summer tromping around her acre of land with her giant goat parading around after her was enough to make him smile wider. He'd like to see that for himself. Actually, he'd love to see that for himself, but the truth was that, this was all surface conversation. It wouldn't go any deeper than that. He was pretty sure she hated him, and he probably had a better chance of being hit by a truck than being invited out to her place to meet her goat. Which was fine. He wouldn't have gone anyway.

"Anyway," she said. "I'm happy out there. How are you doing, Beau? Other than your shoulder needing surgery? How's your family?"

Summer had met Poppy once when she'd come to visit his first year of college. His cousin had been getting ready to graduate with a journalism degree and had already been drifting away from Beau and Cora by that point. But that probably had more to do with her wanting to drift away from her past in general. Poppy had come a long way since her accident, but she'd always be a little fragile because of it. A little broken.

Clearing his throat, Beau hooked his thumbs in his belt loops. "Well, you might have heard that my grandpa passed away a few months ago."

Summer frowned, gazing up at him.

"That's why Poppy, Cora and I are running the shop," he went on. "Well. Running it for now." He always felt the need to emphasize that part. Whether or not people cared didn't matter. He cared. He was here temporarily. Christmas Bay was a nice place to visit but the hometown vibe didn't do anything for him. His parents had left a long time ago, living in different parts of the country now. His grandfather was gone. And if Beau felt any kind of pull toward this place, toward that family vibe, he always shut it down immediately. He liked his life the way it was. Sometimes he had to remind himself of that on long road trips to those obscure places where the biggest fishing tournaments were, but that was okay. Sometimes a man needed a little reminding to keep himself focused and on track. That was normal. That was reality.

"I'm really sorry about your grandpa," Summer said. "I know what a special bond you had."

A woman passed by on the sidewalk, brushing them with her bags. She muttered an apology and he stepped aside, feeling numb.

Beau's grandfather had been more of a father to him than his own father had been. He'd been there when Beau's dad had split, leaving his son reeling. So losing the older man was a wound that still hadn't closed. And maybe it never would. It felt that way sometimes when people offered their condolences. Like the pain would never ease up. It ached, from a place so deep that it was hard to touch most days. He missed his grandpa. He'd give anything to be able to talk to him one last time, to tell him how much he loved him.

"Thank you," he said. His voice sounded husky and he was embarrassed by that. He wasn't used to showing much emotion. But something about standing there on the sidewalk, catching the scent of Summer's hair on the breeze, was making him feel all kinds of messed up.

She clasped her hands in front of her belly and looked down at her shoes. There was really nothing else to say. But at the same time there was so much to say. So much, that a few minutes catching up outside the antique shop would never come close to scratching the surface.

He watched her. It was obvious that he just needed to get on with this. To solidify their business deal and move on. He needed to get back inside the shop and corral this strange feeling inside his chest.

"So," he said. "I'd like to work with you, if you're open to that."

She looked up and smiled. Judging by the expression on her face, she was relieved to be moving on, too.

"I'd definitely be open to that," she said.

"Should we start with these end tables here? And if they go quickly, which they should, I'll call you, and we can talk about the specifics moving forward."

"Great."

She pulled a business card from her pocket and handed it over.

He took it, brushing her fingers in the process.

So that's where this day had ended up. With an old

girlfriend's phone number in his hand and a new business deal that should've made him happy.

But it didn't. Because that strange feeling inside his chest—inside his heart—was growing stronger.

Chapter Two

Summer sat in the cab of her truck, trembling uncontrollably. When Beau walked back inside the antique shop, and she was sure he wouldn't be able to see her, she lay her head back against the rest and let out a shaky breath.

She was annoyed by the shaky breath. And she was annoyed by the trembling. It had been years since she'd last seen Beau, and years since she'd convinced herself that she'd fallen out of love with him. Yeah, she still dreamed about him sometimes, but that was pretty normal, right? And, sure, she thought about him every now and then. When the weather was just right or when she caught the scent of a man's aftershave that reminded her of him.

But she definitely didn't love him anymore. Quite frankly, she didn't even *like* him anymore. He'd proven to be a terrible boyfriend and they hadn't exactly parted on the best terms. But that's what happened when you got dumped. The dumper didn't usually stay in your good graces. But ten years later? It felt like she should be beyond all that now and she really thought she was. Until she'd walked through the door of Earl's Antiques and had turned to see the love of her life—there was no point denying that part, she'd accepted it a long time ago—standing there looking as handsome as ever.

He'd aged some, but in that infuriatingly sexy way that men experienced and women weren't allowed to, at least not in this society. The slight wrinkles around his eyes only made him more attractive. The threads of silver in his blond hair made her want to run her hands through it. And the lines around his mouth made her wonder what it was that he laughed at. And then with a sudden pang of jealousy that didn't even make sense, she caught herself wondering if there was anyone special in his life.

She swallowed hard, looking toward the antique shop and the front door he'd disappeared through. *Hardly.* Anything was possible, but she couldn't really see Beau settled down. He'd been much too selfish for that and, honestly, he still gave off that gruff it's-all-about-me kind of vibe. Maybe it wasn't fair, but that's what she'd come away with. And sure, he'd taken her end tables, which was great, she wasn't going to turn her nose up at that—she needed the business. But if he thought she was going to go all doe-eyed in his presence, he had another thing coming. The fact that she was sitting in her truck now, having to recover from being in his presence, wasn't going to enter into the equation. She didn't care about Beau Evers anymore. She didn't care about his fishing career, she didn't care about his shoulder injury—she *did* care about his grandfather, a man she'd never met, but who had sent her a sweet birthday card once telling her how happy she made Beau—and she certainly didn't care about whether or not he was single. All she cared about was the business her partnership with his antique shop would drum up, and that was it.

Period. Full stop.

Jamming her keys in the ignition, she ignored how it took two tries to get them in there because of her shaking fingers, and started the truck with a roar. She needed a new muffler. Among other things.

No, she didn't care about Beau Evers. She reminded herself of that again as she pulled away from the curb and right into the path of a Jeep that laid on its horn and made her cheeks burn with embarrassment.

Beau's niece Mary frowned, leaning back in one of the chairs in the vet's waiting room and running a hand over Roo's ears. The dog was huge. An Irish wolfhound mix that had been Beau's grandfather's and was now Mary's. Well, technically, she was the antique shop's mascot and belonged to all of them, but Mary was her favorite. She even slept on her bed. Under the covers.

The dog gave Beau some side-eye now, panting and making him feel bad. She hated the vet. But it was a necessary evil. She was being treated for an itchy hot spot and Mary was there for emotional support. Beau was the muscle in the arrangement. He knew from experience that Roo would try to bolt when they walked out the door, and they'd need all the muscle they could get to keep hold of her one hundred and ten pounds.

"So you broke up with her to *fish*?" Mary asked, wrinkling her nose.

Beau could thank Cora for this. She'd peppered him with all kinds of questions last night when he'd mentioned they had a new furniture supplier for the shop.

And it just so happened to be Summer. His Summer. Mary had overheard this and now it was all she wanted to talk about. Apparently, she was fascinated by the fact that her crusty old uncle had ever had a love life at all. He didn't know whether to be amused or offended by that.

"It's complicated," he said, tugging on Roo's leash when she tried to get up to sniff a hissing cat being carried past.

"You guys always say that. You always say 'it's complicated.'" She put air quotes around the words. She was currently a fan of air quotes. "It's not complicated. You have commitment stuff. It's okay, you know. Just admit it."

He looked over, trying not to laugh. He didn't want to encourage her. She was precocious enough as it was.

"You think I've got commitment stuff?"

"Come on, Uncle Beau. Everyone knows. It's nothing to be ashamed of."

"Huh."

"But the first thing you need to do is admit it."

"And why's that?"

"I heard about it on a podcast. About relationships and junk."

"Ah."

"So you broke up with her to fish. And how did that make you feel?"

He raised his brows. "Uh...single?"

"Yes, but did you feel *bad* about it? Did you miss her and stuff?"

She was dead serious. He wondered what podcast this was. Maybe he should tune in sometime. Or not. He was getting enough advice from his niece as it was. In fact, she could probably host her own podcast at this point.

"Yeah," he said. "I missed her. But fishing was my dream. I couldn't have both. Summer and fishing."

"Huh." Mary nodded knowingly.

"What?"

"I'm just saying. I think you *could* have, if you'd *wanted* to. You just didn't *want* to."

Beau shifted in his seat and it squeaked underneath him. The phone rang a few times at the receptionist's desk before being answered by a frazzled-looking woman wearing scrubs with little cats all over them.

"Can we talk about something else?" he said. "And by the way, if you'd like to go into a career in counseling, I'll help with tuition. I think it's right up your alley."

"That's what Mom says. She also says you use humor to detect."

"To detect...you mean deflect."

"Yeah. That."

Beau's neck was hot. This was what happened when you lived in a tiny apartment above your business with your family who happened to be all female. Your personal life got turned into a pet project and you got diagnosed to death. And maybe he was a good candidate for diagnosis, but still. He *really* wanted to talk about something else. In the short amount of time they'd been sitting there, Mary had touched on a few sensitive topics and then some. He'd already been having a hard enough time getting Summer out of his head. And now this. The vet visit from hell. He was starting to feel like poor Roo.

"Look, Uncle Beau," Mary went on. "I get it. Fishing is your thing. But is it going to be your thing forever? I mean, you can't marry a fish. You can't have kids with a fish." She giggled, enjoying the image this must have conjured up.

Beau stared at her. "Exactly what podcast have you been listening to?"

"Oh, good grief! Molly! Molly, get back here!"

He looked over to see a brown-and-white spaniel making her great escape, her collar dangling in her owner's hand.

The receptionist in the cat scrubs lunged for her, but overshot and fell on the floor with an *oomph.* Her bare hands made a thwacking sound on the linoleum and the dog's owner gasped.

"Oh, no! I'm so sorry. Are you okay?"

Beau stood, ready to help her up, but right then the spaniel lunged at Roo. And Roo lunged back.

Beau yanked on her leash and heard a sickening pop. It took a second before he realized it had come from his injured shoulder. Right about the time the pain washed over him like a tsunami.

"Arrrgghh."

His vision went swimmy. Fire roared in the joint like someone had tossed gasoline over it. It climbed up his neck and into his face. He was vaguely aware of Mary standing there, her mouth hanging open, her eyes wide. She was scared to death. Of course she would be, she'd probably never heard anyone make a sound like that before. *He'd* never heard anyone make a sound like that before.

He bit his tongue so hard he tasted blood.

"Molly!" This time the dog's owner tackled her, ending up on the floor alongside the receptionist.

The vet came rushing out, hair flying, glasses askew. "What in the world?"

Roo whined and licked Beau's hand. An apology. But it was too little too late.

"Uncle Beau?"

"I'm alright," he said through gritted teeth. "I'm okay."

But, of course, he wasn't. Something that was probably pretty clear now that there were beads of sweat popping up on his forehead and upper lip.

Mary's eyes filled with tears. "What should we do?"

"We'll call your mom or Aunt Poppy to come get us. I'll need to go to the hospital, but don't worry, alright?"

It was obviously too late for that, as Mary looked vaguely green. He wasn't the only one who'd heard that pop. A sound that bones and joints most definitely shouldn't make, at least not outside of horror movies.

"Oh no," the woman on the floor groaned. She scrambled up to a sitting position alongside the receptionist, and clutched her dog to her chest. A little too tightly, as its poor eyes were bugging from its head. "I'm so sorry. I can drive you?"

Beau tried to hold his arm as still as possible. Partly from the pain, and partly to try and minimize the amount of damage done, if that was even possible. He felt sorry for the woman though, who was the same shade of green as Mary.

The vet came over and took hold of Roo's collar, stroking the dog's head methodically. "Maybe you should let one of us drive you," she said, staring at his arm, and the strange way it was hanging from the joint. "That doesn't look very good. It shouldn't wait."

"I'll call my cousins. If they can't come right away, I'll take a ride. Thanks."

Mary was already on her phone. The vet didn't have to worry, she had no intention of letting anything wait.

"Mom," she said, her voice shaky. "Uncle Beau messed up his shoulder again. It's super gross. He says he needs to go to the hospital. Can you come pick us up?"

If the pain weren't as intense as it was, Beau probably would've chuckled at that. Super gross, indeed. If someone were to write his biography, they could simply sum it up with, *Fisherman. Super gross shoulders.*

Summer opened the gate to Tank's pasture—it was technically a pen, but it was big and grassy, and she didn't like thinking of him in a pen, so she thought of it as a pasture instead—and watched as the big brown goat came barreling down the small hill, bleating as he went.

She laughed, shaking the bucket of alfalfa pellets as he skidded to a stop in front of her, jamming his nose in the bucket like a pig.

Setting it down for him, she fished her phone out of her pocket. She'd been working on a dresser all morning that she thought might be a good fit for Earl's Antiques, and for the last hour she'd been toying with the idea of calling to see if they'd be interested in it. The only thing stopping her was the obvious feeling of warm anticipation at the thought of talking to Beau again. And because that was ridiculous, she shouldn't care either way, she shoved the feeling aside, and reminded herself this was just business. That was it. And *not* calling would be like it was more than just business, and *that* was ridiculous.

Well aware that she was over-thinking the whole

thing, she dialed their number before she could change her mind, and leaned against the fence with her heart beating out a steady rhythm. She needed to get used to talking to him, on the phone and otherwise, if there was a chance they were going to be working together. Calling this morning would normalize their new relationship, and that's all it would do.

The phone rang once, then twice, then three times. Just as she was about to hang up, a woman answered.

"Earl's Antiques, how can I help you?"

Summer cleared her throat and took what she hoped was a steadying breath.

"Yes, hi. My name is Summer Smith, and I restore vintage furniture. I talked to Beau the other day, is he available?"

"Summer," the woman said. Her voice was warm, cheerful. "This is Poppy, remember me?"

Summer smiled, staring out across the pasture with sudden memories flooding her consciousness. She'd met Beau's cousin once and had liked her. Blond, beautiful, incredibly smart. Summer remembered being intimidated by her for about thirty seconds, before the other woman had pulled her into a hug, while gushing over Summer's curls. It had been impossible not to be charmed by her immediately.

"Hi, Poppy," she said. "It's so good to hear your voice. It's been a long time."

"Since college. That feels like a lifetime away."

"Right?"

"Beau told us he'd seen you in the shop the other day. I can't tell you how happy we are about getting to work with you. Your tables are just lovely, Summer. Truly."

"Oh, thank you so much. That means a lot."

There was a pause on the other end of the line, and for a second, Summer thought she might've lost the connection. But then she heard Poppy let out a soft sigh.

"So," the other woman said. "I know you wanted to talk to Beau, but he's kind of out of commission right now."

Summer frowned. "Oh?"

"He was taking our dog to the vet the other day. She's really big. And she lunged at another dog, and he was trying to hold her back, and, well. His poor shoulder is basically toast."

Summer's stomach sank. This wasn't good.

"Was that the shoulder he was going to have surgery on?" she asked. But she already knew the answer. It was obvious from the tone of Poppy's voice.

"The one and only. He had to have an emergency repair on it. And now, we wait."

"Oh no..." Summer rubbed her temple, feeling a little dizzy. She had complicated feelings for Beau. But right then, all she could think about was how hard this was going to be for him.

"There's possible nerve damage," Poppy said quietly. "His fishing career might be over."

The words were like a blow. They made her physically sick. She had no idea how to respond, but luckily, she didn't have to.

"Hey," Poppy said. "A few customers just walked in, I need to run. I'll tell Beau you called, okay? We can catch up soon?"

"Sure, okay. That sounds good. Thanks, Poppy."

And then the line went dead, and Summer blinked into the bright morning sunshine.

She scratched behind Tank's floppy ears and breathed in the comforting smell of him, thinking about what Poppy had said. *His fishing career might be over...*

There had been a time after their breakup when Summer hadn't even been able to stand the word *fishing.* To her, it had stolen her happiness, her love, her future—which hadn't been a great way to look at it; she'd since learned that nobody could steal her happiness if she didn't let them. But she'd been so hurt that she purposely hadn't followed Beau's career, trying to block it out to where the mention of it couldn't wound her all over again. Yet he was such a big deal, an Oregon boy making it big, that it was hard not to know how he'd done over the years. And he'd done really, really well. He'd won tournaments all over the world. Beau was gifted. Most of all, he was passionate. He loved fishing. He'd loved it more than her.

But that was neither here nor there. The point was that it had been his entire life, and now, this person who'd once been her best friend, a man who'd brushed her hair back from her face and told her she was beautiful, might be facing a future without his passion, and that was probably soul-crushing for him.

She didn't want to care about Beau. But the truth was, she cared enough that the thought of his soul being crushed made her unsettled.

Leaning down, she picked up the bucket and tipped it so Tank could get the last of the pellets and told herself that going to see him, especially when he was likely to be in one of the darkest moods of his life, probably wasn't a good idea. Nonetheless, Summer had never adhered much to good ideas. When she'd quit her job, people had told her it wasn't a good idea. Of course they hadn't known that her love of refinishing old furniture hadn't been the entire reason why she'd quit.

When she'd bought her property, her sister and parents had also told her it wasn't a good idea. But Summer was stubborn. She'd needed a fresh start, away from the city.

Away from Eric.

She'd been embarrassed by what had happened between them, humiliated that the police couldn't do anything about it because she hadn't been able to prove much at the time. It felt like they hadn't believed her, but worse, her boss, a trusted mentor, hadn't taken the situation at work seriously, either, and that had been especially hard. Then things had begun to spiral—she'd felt depressed, sad, helpless, scared. She hadn't wanted to end up being the kind of person who was scared all the time, so here she was. In Christmas Bay. The owner of one acre and a goat.

No, seeing Beau probably wasn't a good idea. But it was the right thing to do. He was going to need support. The least she could do was let him know she was there. That she understood. Because, despite everything, despite them growing up and growing apart, she still felt like she knew him very well.

What he did with that was up to him.

Beau glared at the wall. Then looked down at his arm in the sling and glared at that, too. He couldn't even be properly mad at Roo because she'd been lying on his bed, as close to him as she could get, since the minute he'd returned from the hospital.

Sighing, he laid his head back against the headboard. What he wanted was to get the hell out of this bed. Out of Poppy's room, which she'd graciously given up for him. He felt helpless, which he guessed he was, and he hated that. But the surgeon who'd repaired his shoulder—not the fancy one in Portland, it had been too late for that—had told him that his recovery was going to be key. Since his shoulder had already been injured before, there was a possibility of permanent damage now, and how the joint healed in the next few weeks would determine his future in the sportfishing world.

He still couldn't believe his luck. Of all the things he could've been doing, it was holding Roo back from eating a cocker spaniel that had been his downfall. He didn't even have a cool story like falling in some rapids or getting attacked by a bear. And now he was stuck doing nothing, which he'd never been any good at.

He shifted on the bed, prompting Roo to thump her tail a few times. He was supposed to stay still, with his arm propped a certain way, and rest. Eventually he'd be able to move to his grandpa's recliner across the room. And if that went well, he could start moving around slowly. Slow was the word of the day.

Reaching down, he rubbed Roo's ears and tried not to think about what he was going to do if he couldn't go back to fishing. If his casting arm was shot. What would he do? Run the antique shop permanently? He felt his jaw tighten. Not being able to fish was simply too much to contemplate, too much to wrap his head around. Who was he if he wasn't a fisherman?

"Beau?"

He looked up to see Poppy standing there.

"You have a visitor," she said.

"A visitor? I don't know anybody in Christmas Bay anymore."

All his friends were back in Eugene. Or spread across the country, and he only saw them when he was in town for tournaments. And calling them "friends" was a nice way of putting it. They were mostly acquaintances.

Poppy smiled sheepishly. And all of a sudden he knew exactly who she was talking about. *Of course*. This was just like Summer. Sweet, but not taking no for an answer.

"Summer?"

Poppy nodded.

"No." He shook his head. "Tell her I'm not up to it. I don't want to see anyone."

"She said that's what you'd say."

"Good. Then she won't be surprised that she came all the way down here for nothing."

"Beau, come on."

Roo jumped off the bed and shook, making the tags jingle on her collar. At least she was excited about a visitor.

"I'm recovering from surgery here. I'm staying absolutely still and resting, and doing what I'm supposed to be doing."

"Well, I don't think she came over here to jump your bones, if that's what you're thinking."

Beau shot her a look.

"Seriously," Poppy said. "I don't want to tell her to leave, she's so sweet."

She smiled, knowing damn well she was going to get

her way. She and Cora usually got their way with him. Plus, he knew there was an ulterior motive here. They would both think this was romantic. The long-lost girlfriend showing up out of the blue.

"Mary's downstairs asking Summer twenty questions about her goat. You need to let her come up here and say hi, even if it's just to rescue her for a few minutes."

"Alright." He sighed. "But five minutes. Tell her I'm loopy from the drugs or something. Five minutes and then I'm going to pretend to fall asleep."

Ignoring that, she disappeared out the door with Roo trotting along after her.

Beau looked down at himself. He was wearing sweats and a T-shirt, but he felt like he might as well be in his pajamas. He silently cursed his shoulders, both of them, that couldn't seem to stay in their sockets if his life depended on it. If he had to see Summer again, it'd at least be nice to be standing on his own two feet and not looking like something out of *The Walking Dead.*

"Beau?"

He turned his head at the sound of her voice. And there she was. Standing in the doorway. Holding a Tupperware container.

She was so pretty. He found himself looking for just a beat too long.

He let his gaze shift to the container in her hands. Had she remembered his weakness for chocolate-chip cookies? He could smell their sweet warm scent from where he lay, trapped in his bed. Nobody had ever brought him cookies before.

"Summer," he said, remembering that he actually had vocal cords and he should probably use them. "Hi."

"I hope I'm not intruding. But I was in town and thought I'd stop by."

"Nope," he said. "Not at all."

She stood there for a second and an awkward silence settled over them. He pushed himself up, wincing without meaning to.

"Oh. Do you need some help?"

"No," he said quickly. "Nope, I'm fine."

She nodded, not really looking like she believed him, but that was okay. He just needed to get through these next few minutes and then he really was going to pretend to fall asleep. Into a drug-induced nap, like a little old man. She'd never know the difference. Or maybe she would.

"Can I…can I come sit down?"

"Sure."

He watched her walk hesitantly over. Then pull up a chair and sit, holding the container with both hands.

"Are those what I think they are?" he asked.

She set the container on the bedside table. "Just out of the oven."

"Wow. That's sweet, thank you."

"You look like you've kept in shape," she said. "So I'm not sure how much you still indulge in these, but I took a chance."

Her cheeks colored a little and he had the sudden overwhelming urge to reach out and touch them. It took him off guard.

"How are you feeling?" she asked. "Are you in pain?"

Here was his chance. Play up the fact that he was on heavy medication, which made him tired. Really tired.

"Not really. Just dopey from the pain meds."

"Thank goodness for those."

He smiled. And she smiled. And the awkward silence was back.

Poppy appeared in the doorway and they both looked over at the same time.

"Do you guys want some coffee?" his cousin asked. "Or tea?"

"Tea would be lovely," Summer said. "Unless…" Her soft, green-eyed gaze came to rest on Beau again. "Are you too tired to talk for a few minutes? I can go…"

He didn't know if it was the cookies or the sudden offer to leave him alone. Because that's what she had to know he wanted. Since college. Since forever. Which was sad. But he shook his head, surprising himself.

"No, I'm fine." He glanced over at Poppy. "Coffee would be great. Thanks."

"Okey dokey. Coming right up."

And then they were alone again. The sunlight streamed through the window, lighting Summer's hair on fire. Her red curls cascaded around her shoulders, reminding him of a heroine on the cover of a romance novel. Mary was starting to read those. She'd come home from the library the other day with her arms full of them. She'd shown him every single one, giving him a short synopsis of their storylines and why it was that she couldn't wait to dig right in. He had a feeling that curiosity about sex might be part of it. But mostly, Mary was a romantic like her mother and her aunt. She wanted to believe in happily-ever-afters, and that was very sweet. But Beau knew that sometimes ever-afters were just so-so.

"Beau," Summer began quietly, "I hope you don't mind that I'm here."

"I don't mind."

"I knew you might not want to see anyone. But you know me, I kind of barrel ahead anyway."

Yes, he knew. It had been one of the things that he'd loved most about her. Her stubbornness. Her tenacity.

And then some memories came back. Of them wrestling on his bed in his dorm room, playing and laughing and breathless. That year with Summer had been full of breathlessness and color. Like Mary had asked, why hadn't he been able to love Summer *and* fishing? But he also knew that a darkness had already begun to creep into his personality by then, a general distrust of people and circumstance. He'd witnessed his mother grieving the lost relationship with his father, never forgiving herself for the breakdown of their marriage. Gradually sinking into a decline of alcohol and bitterness.

Summer coming into Beau's life had been like the sun coming out briefly during a storm. And then the clouds had engulfed him again and he'd had to focus on the surest things, the things that would never go away. And that had been fishing. Except it had gone away, hadn't it? In the form of two broken-down shoulders and a body that felt old before its time.

"I just want you to know," she said, "that I'm here if you need to talk. Or if you need anything at all."

"You just want me to buy more of your furniture."

She laughed. "You got me. That's it."

He remembered that laugh.

"They sold, by the way," he said. "The end tables we took. They're already gone. I was going to call you, and then this..."

"Oh yeah?"

He could tell she was trying not to show how happy she was about that. He wondered how well she did with this furniture business. If it paid the bills pretty well or if she lived month to month. She had a house and some property, so she had to be doing okay, but still. He wondered. It took guts to walk away from your job and follow your dreams. He'd walked away from her and followed fishing, so maybe he was courageous as well. He doubted that, but it was a nice change from feeling like he'd made a mistake all those years ago. Like he'd been a coward.

Silence settled over them again and he stared at the wallpaper and she seemed fascinated by the pattern on his bedspread.

And then Poppy reappeared, like some sort of angel meant to save him from himself. She held two steaming mugs and handed one of them to Summer with a smile.

"Careful. It's hot."

"Thanks so much."

"I didn't know if you took sugar or not, but here are a few packets, just in case."

She handed Beau his coffee. He took his black.

"Thanks," he said.

Without another word, she disappeared again.

Summer took a careful sip of her tea then held it in her lap, the steam curling into the air like a potion.

"Thank you—"

"I like—"

Beau smiled. "Go ahead."

"Oh. I just wanted to say that I like your apartment. It's so cool that there's an entire living area up here."

He looked around. "Yeah. It's small, but there's room for everyone. Even the dog, and she's giant."

"I met her when I came in. Oh my gosh, she's amazing. How much does she weigh, anyway?"

"One hundred and ten pounds. On the dot." He pointed to his shoulder. "Know how I know?"

"Oh no."

"Turns out that massive dogs and weak shoulder sockets don't mesh very well."

She winced. "I'm sorry, Beau."

"Yeah, well..."

They grew quiet again and Beau took a sip of his coffee. Needing something to do with his free hand.

"What were you going to say?" she asked.

He raised his brows.

"Just now."

"Oh... I was going to thank you for coming. It was nice of you. Especially since..."

Damn it. With two carelessly chosen words he'd pushed the door to the past wide open, and that was a place he didn't care to visit. He did enough of that in his own head. Regretting things. Trying to convince himself that he'd had his reasons. But then Summer had to go showing up with two refinished end tables, reminding him exactly what he'd walked away from. How good he'd had it for a while.

"I don't hate you," she said. "If that's what you're thinking."

"I'm not thinking anything."

He watched her and she watched him back. There was a steeliness behind her eyes. She was sweet, but she wasn't *that* sweet.

"What?" he asked after a minute.

"I don't know, Beau. Just that you've never been very good at saying how you really feel."

"It's been a long time. Maybe I've changed."

He couldn't believe he just said that. He hadn't changed. If anything, he'd gotten worse.

"Well, that'd be a good thing," she said.

"Was I that bad?"

She just looked at him. His face heated. She'd always been able to press his buttons. Force him to look at things he'd rather not. Maybe that's why he'd broken up with her. Maybe it hadn't had anything to do with fishing at all.

"I've forgiven you, Beau," she said. "It's all in the past. We're starting fresh with this business deal and—"

"Whoa, whoa, whoa." He set his coffee down. "You've forgiven me?"

"I have."

"Summer. I mean, come on. I never cheated on you. I never led you astray. I was honest about what I wanted from the beginning."

"Are you serious?"

"That's how I remember it."

"And that's your problem. You're rewriting history to fit a narrative you're more comfortable with. We were talking about moving in together."

"What?" He shook his head. "No. Nope. That was never on the table."

Great. *Super.* This was going swell. But he couldn't seem to shut his mouth. He did remember talking about moving in together, actually. He remembered it very well because he'd woken up the next morning scared to death. Ready to run. And then he had.

"You're insufferable, Beau Evers," she said softly.

"Thank you?"

"You don't get to tell me what happened. I *know* what happened. I lived through it."

"We weren't together that long."

She stared at him. It made his heartbeat slow a fraction. He wished he could suck the words back in. They'd been bad, even for him. But this was his way. It protected him from getting divorced like his parents or breaking into pieces like Poppy. It was how he hadn't been hurt back then, and it was how he wasn't going to be hurt now. Letting Summer back into his life, even for a business deal, had been stupid. It was clear he wasn't over her, even now, and he had to focus on getting better. It was as simple as that.

She set her tea on the table next to his coffee. It had cooled some and the steam had disappeared, which was fitting, because Summer had cooled, too.

"Maybe this wasn't such a good idea," she said.

"Maybe it wasn't."

"I thought we'd grown up. I thought you'd be better. I was wrong about that."

He felt the muscles in his back tighten, sending a shooting pain through his shoulder. He forced himself to relax but the pain remained, throbbing and biting, punishing him perfectly for how he was. How he'd always been.

She stood and he caught her scent.

And then she was gone. He guessed that had been his goal this entire time.

He swallowed hard, staring at the wall. The room was empty and quiet, and other than the lingering scent of her perfume, it was like she'd never been there at all.

Mission accomplished.

Chapter Three

Summer made her way down the stairs, fury blurring her vision. She thought she'd been so nice coming over to let him know someone understood how he was feeling. But that was the problem. She'd never really understood how Beau was feeling, despite thinking she did, and despite wanting to so badly. To assume she did now had been a massive error in judgment. She guessed she shouldn't be surprised this visit had ended the way it had, but she was anyway. That's what she got for being optimistic.

Coming to the last of the stairs, she looked around the shop, hoping Poppy was busy with customers. She didn't see her but the dog, Roo, came sauntering over with her long tail waving like a flag. She nudged Summer in the thigh, demanding attention.

Summer reached down to give her a scratch. "Good girl, Roo," she whispered. "You're a very good girl."

After a few seconds, she gave the dog a final pat and then made her way toward the front door. If she hurried, she might be able to make it out without being spotted.

"Leaving so soon?"

Her stomach sank as she turned with a smile on her

lips. She wasn't sure she'd be able to fake this one. She was still too mad and probably would be for the rest of the day. It definitely wasn't Poppy's fault, though, so she made sure to smile a little wider than necessary. Then realized it was probably too wide. Too forced. Too obvious. She realized this right about the time she felt tears stinging her eyes. *Great.*

Poppy had been smiling, too, but when she saw the look on Summer's face, it withered. "What happened? Did Beau say something to upset you?"

Summer wasn't sure how much to tell her. And then decided it didn't matter. Truth be told, she probably wasn't going to be working with Earl's Antiques after this. That ship had sailed. Seeing Beau regularly would be too hard. Life was too short and there were other shops, other businesses, that would be happy to have her furniture. Even if money was kind of tight right now. Even if her last electric bill had almost made her choke on her coffee. It'd be fine. She had a second job as a barista on the weekends. She'd make it.

"To be honest," she said. "Yeah. He did."

Poppy sighed. "Oh boy. I'm sorry."

"No, don't be sorry. It's not your fault."

"He can be a lot. And then, with this injury and the fishing...well. You know."

Oh, she knew alright.

"I should've expected it," Summer said. "And I guess I did, but I came anyway. Dumb."

"I just hope this won't spoil working with us."

"About that..."

Poppy frowned. "Oh no."

"It's just that I'm not sure I can do this. I thought I

was over Beau, and I am," she said quickly. "But maybe I'm not over how things ended between us, and I'm not sure seeing him again will be good for me. I'm trying to get my business up and running, and I need to put all my energy into that. Beau is a…distraction."

Poppy nodded. "What if you didn't deal with Beau? What if you dealt with me or Cora instead?"

It was a nice offer, but one that Summer knew wouldn't work. And Poppy probably did, too. The shop was too small. The way Summer understood it, Poppy and Cora were busy with their own branches of the business. Beau was the furniture and antiques buyer. He was the one she'd need to work with long-term and she couldn't stand the thought of anything long-term with Beau Evers at the moment. What she'd said was true—all her focus needed to be on her business. She needed only positive vibes, and Beau was the opposite of positive anything.

Poppy reached out and pulled her into a quick hug. "It's okay. I get it, believe me. But keep us in mind for the future?"

Summer nodded, emotional and not wanting to be emotional. She wanted to be detached, like Beau was. But that wasn't how she was built. When she loved, she loved hard.

"You're sweet," she said. "I'll definitely keep you in mind."

Giving the other woman a parting smile, she turned and headed for the door. So with Earl's Antiques not working out, she'd have to pick up some more hours at the coffee stand. Maybe they'd have some night shifts. She'd be tired from working in the shop all day, but if this was what it took to keep from going back to an office job, it was exactly what she'd do.

She walked out the door with her chin up. But with her heart straining under the weight of seeing Beau again. Of remembering something special and tender inside of him, despite everything—something that most people never got to see, but that she'd been privy to at one point in her young life. And of saying goodbye to him for the last time.

He was a royal jerk, but he was still the love of her life.

Still.

Beau pulled his windbreaker on carefully, his shoulder aching. He'd just had his third physical therapy appointment and he was starting to worry that the feeling, not to mention the strength, wouldn't ever come back to his arm. At this rate, he didn't have to wait for the follow-up appointment with the surgeon; he knew sportfishing was off the table. Especially since his other shoulder was a goner, too.

It was a realization that had put him into a funk over the last two weeks. He didn't want to talk to anyone. He didn't want to see anyone. He didn't want to work—although he kind of had to do that. Cora and Poppy needed his help if they all wanted to pay the bills and keep the momentum they'd worked so hard to build. It was important that he pitch in, and he was, but his attitude was garbage.

"It was nice seeing you again, Mr. Evers," the receptionist said from behind the front desk. She gave him a smile. Her dark eyes sparkled and he could tell she was trying to flirt with him. She'd been trying since that first appointment, but he'd been in his own world.

"Yeah," he said. "Thanks. You too."

"I hope you don't mind me asking," she said, "but aren't you that sport fisherman?"

Beau had just given her his copay and he tucked his credit card back in his wallet. Normally, the general public didn't know fishermen from Adam. Even pretty famous sport fishermen—or were they fisher people? There were several women on the circuit that had given him a run for his money. But Beau had made it pretty big and he was from this neck of the woods, so the locals recognized him sometimes.

He smiled back. Having his shoulder basically nonfunctional sucked. Not being able to fish sucked. But this part definitely didn't suck. Who didn't enjoy a little attention from attractive women with stars in their eyes?

"Yup," he said. "That's me."

"My dad watches ESPN all the time. You're on quite a bit."

Correction. I used *to be on quite a bit. Before this injury. Now there are about fifty up-and-coming young guys ready to take my place.*

"Anyway," she said, lowering her lashes and looking a little shy. "He's a big fan. Maybe I could get your autograph for him sometime."

"Do you have something I can write on? I can give it to you now if you want."

"Really?"

"Sure. What's his name?"

She handed over a pad of paper. "Walter. He'll be so happy."

Beau scribbled out his usual *Happy fishing, Walter! Best wishes, Beau Evers.*

He handed it back to the now-grinning receptionist. She really was pretty. If he had any gumption at all, he'd be taking this golden opportunity to ask her out. He didn't see a ring. Plus, the flirting. But was he interested in anything other than a few dates? No. He'd been there, done that, and he was still recovering, quite frankly. Then again, a few dates, and maybe getting to second base if she was game, might help him move on from Summer. At least while she was stuck in his head and he was stuck in Christmas Bay. Both of which were looking more and more like long-term prospects.

"You know," he said, "if you're not—"

His phone rang from his back pocket and he pulled it out, meaning to send it straight to voicemail. But when he saw Cora's name flash across the screen, he worried it was some kind of emergency. Ever since Poppy's accident, emergencies were his first thought whenever the phone rang. An unfortunate side effect of childhood trauma.

"Sorry," he said. "I just need to take this really quick."

The receptionist gave him a slightly disappointed look as he stepped away from the desk.

"Hello?"

"Hey," Cora said. "Where are you?"

"At the physical therapist. Why? Everything okay?"

"Everything's fine. But we have a little problem. Well, I guess it's not a *problem.* It's actually great news, but it does involve Summer and I know how things went the other day..."

Beau's heart dropped, just like it always did when

someone mentioned Summer. He made up his mind that when he got off this phone call, he was definitely going to ask the receptionist with the dark, sparkling eyes out. He was going to take her to dinner, and he was going to kiss her good-night if it seemed like she wanted him to, and he was going to move on from Summer Smith for good this time.

Walking to an empty corner of the waiting room, he switched the phone to his other ear. "Yeah, it wasn't great."

Poppy had already told him that Summer wasn't planning on working with Earl's Antiques anymore, courtesy of him. His cousin had been more than a little annoyed. Actually, both his cousins had been annoyed, and Mary had called him a grump again for good measure. He guessed he deserved it.

"We're going to need you to smooth things over," Cora said matter-of-factly. "Go over to her house, kiss her feet, kiss her goat's feet, whatever it takes."

"Goats don't have feet. They have hooves." He pinched the bridge of his nose.

"Whatever. Just pucker up, Beau."

He looked out the window, where an elderly man was heading up the front steps. His gray hair was perfectly combed and he wore a bright yellow sweatshirt that said Life is Better With a Schnauzer!

"If I'm going to kiss anyone's feet," he said, "it's not going to be Summer's. Or her goat's."

"Get over yourself, cousin."

"Why? What's so important that I have to make friends with Summer again?"

"I'll just point out that things were going fine before you went and messed them up."

"Are you gonna tell me what's going on here," he said, "or am I going to have to guess?"

"You know those end tables that we got from her?"

"Yeah."

"Well, some hoity-toity lady bought them. An old customer of Grandpa's."

"I know."

"You don't know who she is though."

"Who is she?" He was getting tired of this conversation. He hadn't had lunch yet and he was hungry. Plus, he had people to ask out. A personal life to attend to.

"Apparently, she just bought that big mid-century modern mansion in Eugene where all those presidents and actors stayed in the fifties and sixties. It used to be some oil tycoon's house and then it was empty for a long time and, just recently, this lady bought it. She's going to do a huge remodel on it, historically accurate. I read about it in the newspaper. Anyway, she bought the end tables and she came back this morning. She wants the entire house furnished in Summer's pieces. The *entire* house."

Beau stared out the window. "That would take forever. Summer doesn't have that kind of inventory."

"I know, and I told her that, and she doesn't care. She said she can wait. She seems a little eccentric. Definitely well off. Money doesn't seem to be an issue, and she wants what she wants. She likes shopping with us, she had a loyalty to Grandpa, and she wants Summer's pieces."

Beau rubbed the back of his neck. "Okay. But why

can't she just go directly to Summer if she wants them that badly?" As soon as he'd said it, he realized how dumb that was. It was a kneejerk response made because he wanted to keep his distance.

Sure, this lady *could* go directly to Summer. Technically. But that would cut Earl's Antiques out completely. And why do that when they'd had a perfectly good thing going before he'd gone and messed it up? Cora's words, not his.

"Are you kidding? This could be huge for us. It's worth a little finessing on our end, don't you think?"

"You mean it's worth a little foot kissing."

"Exactly."

He never should've answered the phone. If Cora had had a flat tire or something, she could've called AAA. Now, he was having to consider not only seeing Summer again, but having to *finesse* her, at that.

Still, he needed to try. If this deal was as good as Cora was making it sound, it would provide financial stability for his cousins, who were counting on him right now. It was the kind of deal that could keep them well in the black for months to come. And that was a very good thing.

"Beau?" Cora said. "Are you there?"

"I'm here."

"And?"

"I don't want to do this."

"Why? Afraid you might fall in love with her again?"

Beau scowled. "Why would I do that?"

"I don't know. Because it was pretty easy the first time?"

That was the last time he was going to get drunk and

confide in his cousins about anything. He couldn't remember exactly what he'd told them that night over Thai take-out and dirty martinis, but it didn't matter. It had obviously been enough.

"Whatever," he mumbled.

"We need this, Beau. You know we do."

Yeah, he knew.

"Fine," he bit out. "*Fine.* I'll do it."

"Thank you! It'll all work out, I promise. And after it's done, if you don't ever want to see Summer again, you won't have to. Easy-peasy."

Right. That's exactly what he'd thought the last time she'd walked out the door, her red hair glowing in the afternoon light. He'd been trying so hard to block it out, but he remembered how it had felt to touch it, to touch *her*. That was the thing about Summer—she kept coming back again and again. The thought of her, the sweetest memories of her.

Just like a boomerang, straight to his heart.

Summer tied the cranberry-red apron around her waist and looked out the window of French Vanilla, the one and only coffee stand in Christmas Bay, watching as the fireball sun sank toward the ocean in the distance. This was what she got for coming in to talk to her supervisor, a pretty blonde named Avery, who couldn't have been more than nineteen-years-old, if that. She should've called. Instead, she'd come down and had been roped into working tonight for Avery, who'd scored last-minute concert tickets in Portland.

"But more hours?" Summer asked again as Avery

rushed around grabbing her things, her hair falling like a curtain of silk over one shoulder. "I hate to ask but—"

"Oh, I know. It's okay, hon." Avery called everyone "hon." Summer was no exception. "I got you. I'll put you down for more hours."

"But they have to be in the evenings or on weekends, I work in my shop during the day."

"Oh yeah. Right. Your furniture thingy?"

Summer smiled patiently. Her "furniture thingy" was what paid her mortgage, but since the deal with Earl's Antiques had fallen through, she was going to have to lean on her coffee gig pretty hard until she could get her feet underneath her. But she knew Avery wasn't really interested in the specifics. Something that seemed clear as the younger woman opened a small pink compact and applied a fresh coat of lip gloss.

"And thanks a ton for working tonight," Avery said, rubbing her lips together with a smack. "I mean, Ariana Grande, are you *kidding* me?"

She pulled on a fitted denim jacket, the sleeves of which wouldn't fit past Summer's own wrists.

"Have a good time. Be careful."

"Oh, for sure," Avery said and yanked her into a hug that smelled like the Gap. "Don't worry about washing the windows and the floor. I'll do those in the morning."

"Okay."

"Byeeee!"

Summer watched her run out to her Kia and climb inside, promptly rolling the windows down and turning her stereo up so it thumped through the small parking lot. It reminded Summer of her college days. Days when she and Beau would go out to the river, have a cold beer and talk about their future. Except they hadn't ended up having one of those, had they? It had just been a bunch of talk; at least, it had been for him. Even now, watching Avery pull away, her taillights burning through the dusk, Summer found herself longing for that feeling. That love that she hadn't been able to hold on to.

She turned away with a sigh, resigned to cleaning the little stand, starting with the windows because they were smudged and it would be less for Avery to have to do in the morning. She worked that way for the next hour until the cars driving through dwindled to almost nothing and an eerie darkness settled outside. There was no moon tonight—it was choked out by the storm clouds overhead—and a low wind whistled through the evergreens on the edge of the parking lot.

Leaning forward to lower the blinds, Summer watched as a dark SUV slowed then came to a stop near the stand, its headlights cutting through the gritty night. It sat there idling and she frowned. If they wanted coffee, they probably would've pulled through by now. It wasn't unusual for her to open up for someone if they'd just caught her at closing, and a lot of the locals knew that. But this was a car she didn't recognize, which didn't mean much. It could be a tourist, and probably was. Maybe they were lost or something.

But for some reason, it felt strange. She knew Christmas Bay's chief of police, Ben Martinez, and he was a nice guy. He'd given the girls at the stand his card and told them to call any time, day or night, if there were any weirdos lurking around. Even with Summer's history with Eric, she hadn't ever used his number. She hadn't felt like she'd needed to. Since coming to live in Christmas Bay, she'd felt fairly secure, happy in the knowledge that he didn't know where she was. Or he wasn't *supposed* to know, that is.

Now, as she narrowed her eyes at the SUV, she thought about dialing the police department and asking for someone to drive by. The thought of walking out to her car by herself tonight wasn't exactly thrilling her. Better to be safe than murdered.

Just as she was getting ready to dig her phone out of her purse, the SUV backed slowly up and then turned around. She watched it idle in the darkness for a few seconds before it pulled out onto the highway, and was gone in a flash of blood-red taillights.

Summer took a deep breath. Maybe she watched too much *Dateline*. She thought of Beau and how safe she'd always felt with him, but that was before he'd broken her heart.

The momentary feeling of sadness passed, though, just like it usually did. She was single, and she was strong and capable. Sure, Eric had freaked her out, but she was safe now and he was a distant memory.

But as she grabbed her purse and flipped the lights off, she had to acknowledge the tiny feeling in her gut that told her to stay on her toes anyway.

Just in case.

Chapter Four

Beau drove down the highway with the windows down, the cool coastal breeze blowing against his bare arms. His truck was a stick shift, so he'd had to borrow Poppy's Subaru—an electric-blue, four-wheel drive that she'd bought a few months ago. It fit in better in Christmas Bay than her sleek black Mercedes had. Beau had to hand it to his cousin—she'd made the transition to small town life well. She was even in a relationship with Justin Frost who owned the hardware store across the street.

It was a pretty big deal, the fact that they were together, since Justin's little brother, Danny, had been Poppy's boyfriend in high school—the one who'd been killed in the car accident that had shaken the entire town. But Poppy and Justin had found a way to come together again, bonding over their shared grief. They'd moved forward through forgiveness and grace. And then they'd fallen in love. Poppy had come a long way since moving here. She was settling in, and Beau was happy for her. She deserved all the happiness.

But he, on the other hand, was still fighting this move tooth and nail. It had been hard enough losing his grandfather. But losing fishing, too? And then having to see

Summer again. Well…that was proving to be more than he could comfortably handle.

He watched the road ahead, a log truck roaring past in the oncoming lane and rattling the little car in its wake. He breathed in the smell of exhaust and pavement and sea air, and wondered again how he'd ended up here. Not just back where he'd grown up, which really was coming full circle, but back to denying how he felt about a woman who had the power to turn his world upside down. He thought he'd put a nail in that particular coffin years ago. Yet, here he was. Driving out to her place. He'd had to ask around, but it hadn't been hard to find out where she lived—that was a small town for you.

He looked over at his GPS and saw that he was less than a mile away. He still wasn't sure what he was going to say when he got there. Cora had told him to beg. He wouldn't go that far, but he'd definitely turn on the charm to get Summer to reconsider their business deal. He was pretty confident he could be charming if he had to be.

His phone vibrated from the dash. He was getting close. The air out here smelled sweet, like grass and flowers. And salty, of course, like the sea. If he looked hard enough, he could catch glimpses of the water on the horizon, the azure blue mixing with the earth tones of the dunes and beach. He breathed deeply, bracing himself for seeing her again.

And then, suddenly, there she was. Standing in front of her mailbox by the highway, looking down at an open letter in her hands. Her hair was tied up in a red bandana, and she wore a pair of overalls spattered with paint. He slowed and turned on his blinker, aware that his mouth had gone dry. The overalls were big and chunky, revealing little, but there was nothing wrong with Beau's memory and he knew exactly what she looked like underneath.

She didn't even look up when he turned into her driveway. She kept staring down at the letter, her body rigid.

He pulled up to her front porch, the gravel crunching underneath the Subaru's tires, and turned off the engine. The house was cute—a little white farmhouse with a wraparound front porch. Hanging baskets full of purple and pink petunias rocked in the breeze, along with an old porch swing with cheerful throw pillows tucked in the corners.

Looking over at Summer, he climbed out of the car and stuck the keys in his pocket. It was only then that she glanced up, her gaze coming to rest on him as if she were emerging from a trance.

"Beau? What are you doing here?"

He walked toward her. She wore a fitted white tank top underneath her overalls. Like her face, her arms were freckled, and as he got closer, he could smell her sunscreen.

"I came to talk to you," he said.

She dropped the letter to her side.

"Is now not a good time?"

She stared at him. Then folded the letter quickly and tucked it back in the envelope. "It's fine."

She didn't seem thrilled to see him. But why would she be? Still, he wondered fleetingly what it would be like to have someone like her, somewhere like this to come home to. To have her run into his arms and kiss his neck—tell him she'd missed him. And all of a sudden, that image felt like a punch to the gut.

"Are you alright? You seem…"

"I'm fine," she said. Then began walking toward her shop.

There was a small pasture across from it, where a fat brown goat grazed in the sun. Presumably, Tank.

"What do you want to talk about?" she asked, setting a brisk pace.

He had to jog to catch up. "Our business deal."

"What business deal? That didn't work out, remember?"

"Well, technically, we didn't give it a chance to work."

She looked over, cocking an eyebrow. "'We'?"

"Okay. *I* didn't give it a chance."

"Right."

"But I was hoping you might reconsider."

"Why would I do that?"

She was walking fast, and he was out of shape. A few weeks in a recliner hadn't done anything for his lung capacity.

"Can you slow down?" he asked, out of breath. "Still healing, remember?"

"You look like you're getting along pretty well." But she slowed anyway. Even if she wasn't gorgeous, he could've kissed her for that.

He came to a stop and took a deep breath. "My God, woman. Are you training for a marathon?"

She gave him a hint of a smile. "You never could keep up."

"Yeah, and I'm old now, so…"

"Thirty isn't old."

"Tell that to my shoulders."

"Injured, not old."

"Speaking of thirty, your birthday is coming up, isn't it?"

If she was surprised that he remembered, she didn't show it.

"We're talking about your age, not mine," she said, her eyes twinkling.

They'd always been good at sparring. But they'd been better at making up.

"How is your shoulder doing, anyway?" she asked.

"Not great. Not really sure what the future looks like. Fishing kind of requires a functioning arm."

He hadn't meant to add that last part. It had just slipped out. And now she was looking at him with a sympathetic expression and he wanted to kick himself. He wasn't there to have a heartfelt conversation. He was there to try to get her to work with him again.

"I'm sorry, Beau."

"I'll be okay."

They stood there for a few seconds, the sun warm on their shoulders. He looked down at the letter she was holding. He was curious about it and he also wanted to steer the subject away from himself.

"What's that all about?" he asked. "It seemed like you barely heard me drive up."

She shoved it into her pocket. "Nothing."

"I don't believe that."

She sighed. "Remember that old coworker I told you about?"

He remembered. The one she'd had a thing with. Beau didn't like to think of Summer having a *thing* with anyone. It was like they'd just broken up. Or worse, were still together. The thought made his gut twist with a feeling uncomfortably close to envy.

"It's from him," she said. "Well, I think it's from him. It's not signed. Long story."

"I've got time if you want to tell it."

For a second, he thought she was going to. But then she turned and began walking toward the shop again, this time slower. He fell into step beside her.

"Another time," she said.

"Okay."

"Wow. That's not the Beau Evers I know. Taking no for an answer."

"I'm trying to be respectful."

"You were always respectful. But when you wanted something..."

"I know. I didn't stop. Still don't stop."

"No, you don't. And that's why you're here, right?"

That was why he was there. He hoped that was *all* he was there for. He hadn't been able to stop thinking about Cora's warning the other day—the one about him falling in love again. He was vulnerable when it came to Summer, there was no doubt about that. But he liked to think he had control over his emotions now. He was a grown man, after all. Not the boy who'd dated her back then. Some people might say he'd gotten callous but... whatever. The most important thing was that he wasn't going to make the same mistake twice.

His jaw clenched at that thought. Even he, with all his obvious faults and shortsightedness, couldn't call loving Summer a mistake.

They came to a stop in front of her shop and she opened the door.

"Want to come in?" she asked. "See what I'm working on?"

"There you go again. Trying to push furniture on me."

"You've got my number."

"I'm a master at understanding the human psyche."

She laughed.

"That's funny?"

"Yes, Beau. That's definitely funny."

Putting his hands in his pockets, he leaned back on his heels. "Well, let's see what you've got in there. Then maybe I'll see something that I can't resist and I'll be able to talk you into working with me again."

She gave him a look. He had no idea if she planned on giving him another chance. Maybe she was going to make him work for it. It was a fitting thought as he followed her inside and looked around.

It was a small cozy space. There was a box fan in the corner, moving the air around, so it was warm but not stuffy. The soft overhead lighting was concentrated on the center of the shop where a beautiful old dresser sat in the process of being stripped. The natural blond wood looked soft and feathery to the touch and the smell of sawdust permeated his senses. An old transistor radio on the workshop bench was tuned to something from the seventies, the tinny voice of the nameless musician filling the space with nostalgia. He wasn't surprised that Summer would be listening to a throwback station, from a radio of all things, instead of her iPhone and some Bluetooth speakers. She'd always been an old soul. Something else he'd always loved about her.

"Well," she said, burying her hands in her overall pockets, "here it is. Not fancy, but it gets the job done."

No, it wasn't fancy. It was simple and rustic, and it fit her personality perfectly.

"This is the dresser you were talking about?"

She nodded. "I got it from an estate sale. It had a few coats of paint on it, so it's taken a while to get down to the maple, but I think it's lovely."

He looked back at her and felt his chest constrict a little. "Yeah," he said. "Lovely."

They stood there for a few seconds, the music coming from the radio switching to an artist he recognized. Karen Carpenter. His grandfather would love that.

He cleared his throat. "So. I'd like that dresser."

She smiled.

"I'd like that dresser," he continued, "and I'd like you to reconsider working with us."

Her expression was unreadable and again he wondered how hard he was going to have to work for this.

"I don't know, Beau," she said. "We're like oil and water, you and me."

He wasn't sure what to say to that. The words, not exactly untrue, were sharp nonetheless. He'd always thought they were different but not impossibly so. The reason they hadn't stayed together was because of his issues, not because they weren't good together. And the fact that he was defensive of this wasn't lost on him, either.

"I wouldn't go *that* far," he said evenly.

"Really?"

"Really."

"I don't want to rehash our relationship, Beau. Or

we'll end up exactly where we were the other day. With me walking away and you feeling bad afterward."

She pretty much had his number there.

"I'm not so sure," he said with a shrug. "I'm thinking maybe if you got some things off your chest, we might be able to start fresh."

She raised her brows.

"It's a business deal," he said. "Something that will benefit us both. So talking it out wouldn't be such a bad thing. And, yeah, maybe I do feel bad about the other day. About what I said."

He wasn't used to admitting when he was wrong. He sure hadn't done much of it when they were together. Trying to smooth things over after they'd had a fight, and admitting he was usually to blame for those fights, were two different things.

"So why don't we clear the air?" he said.

"That would take a lot longer than a five-minute conversation. If we're being honest."

"Okay. I get that. How long do you think we need?"

"You're serious."

"Dead serious."

"You must really like my furniture."

"I do," he said. "And I like selling your furniture. It's popular, which you should know. That means a good return for the shop, and for you. Win, win."

She nodded.

"So," he said. "How long do we need?"

She was clearly thinking about it. Deciding whether or not to humor him, no doubt. He thought again about the pretty receptionist at his physical therapist's office and how he'd been so anxious to ask her out. He never had.

After he'd hung up the phone with Cora that day, he'd gone out to his car without saying anything to the brunette behind the front desk, and that bothered him. He'd had it all planned out. He'd even decided on where he was going to take her if she'd said yes—a seafood place in Newport that had been in the May issue of *Coastal Monthly.* He'd been ready to pull out all the stops, impress her with his chivalry.

But he hadn't ended up doing a damn thing.

He let his gaze drop to Summer's mouth, her lips glistening underneath the shop's warm lighting. And he wondered if she'd had anything to do with that. Obviously, if that was the case, he needed to get a handle on it right now. And spending more time with her, talking about what he'd done wrong all those years ago, wasn't the best way to get a handle on anything. The *best* way would be to let her walk out of his life again, business deal be damned. But he had people depending on him. *Family* depending on him. He had a career to try to get back to, and he needed to make a living up until that point. A partnership with Summer was the best way to make that happen.

So he was going to have to get a grip on these feelings while trying to get back in her good graces again, which was going to be tricky. Not being a jerk would have to be paramount, of course. He could almost hear Mary chirping in his ear. *And don't be a grump!*

"Okay," she finally said. "Why don't we go out for coffee and we can talk about the logistics? We don't have to air out all our dirty laundry, but we should be honest with each other about what to expect from a partnership, and how that's going to look. Maybe we'll decide it's best to leave well enough alone."

"And maybe we'll decide not to."

"You're not usually such an optimist."

"Well, no," he said. "But this is different."

"This is business."

"Exactly."

To Beau, it sounded like they were trying to convince themselves. And maybe they were. For all he knew, Summer had the same reservations he did. Could she be worried about falling for him, too? He doubted it, but anything was possible.

"Alright," she said. "Coffee then?"

"Coffee."

"I'll be working in the evenings for a while, so it'll have to be in the afternoon."

"Why evenings?"

"I'm a barista," she said. "It's helping pay the bills until I can count on the business more…"

He'd been wondering how well she did refinishing furniture, if it was enough to live on, and she'd answered his question. Maybe it was enough when things were going well, but if they were unstable at all…

He watched her with a newfound respect. She'd always hustled, but this was especially impressive. She was making a go of it, and she was making a go of it alone. Having your own business was risky, he knew that from years of watching his grandfather run the shop. It took guts to do what she was doing.

"Any day but Tuesdays and Thursdays work for me," he said. "Physical therapy."

She glanced down at his arm, which he'd started rubbing. It ached, especially after his appointments, but he was getting used to the discomfort. It didn't bother him nearly as much as the questions it represented. The uncertainty.

"How's that going?" she asked. "The therapy?"

"It's going."

"Going well?"

"It's...going."

She nodded, obviously expecting more of an answer. But the thing was, he was afraid that if he started talking about these things—telling her how hard his therapy was, how much he was struggling with it and that he was scared to death of not being able to go back to doing the only thing he knew how to do—he wouldn't be able to shut up. That he'd be a floodgate of pent-up *stuff* and she'd look at him like she had a few minutes ago—with sympathy in her eyes. And the thought of that was too much to take.

He took a full breath and tried again. "It's hard," he said evenly. "My range of motion sucks and the strength just isn't there. At least, not anywhere near where I need it to be. But the therapist said consistency with the exercises is key, so that's what I'm doing. My exercises, and trying to be positive. At least, as positive as I can manage, which, you know, isn't that positive."

Her lips tilted. Her expression lifted a little.

So this was how he let people in? Simple, really. But inside it felt like he'd nudged a door open that was supposed to stay closed. It was supposed to protect him and now he felt the drafty cold from the other side whisper against his heart, chilling it. A warning sign.

"Anyway," he said quickly. "That's how it's going. When can you meet for coffee?"

She pulled out her phone and while she checked her calendar, he walked over to the dresser to take a closer look. But what he really wanted was to move farther away from Summer. A woman who'd come back into his life and managed to turn it upside down in just a matter of days.

Chapter Five

Summer bent down to slip her shoes and socks off, eager to feel the cool, wet sand ooze between her toes. Her best friend Angie had taken hers off a few minutes ago and had rolled her jeans up to walk in the lapping waves. It was a gorgeous afternoon—sunny and fairly warm for the Oregon Coast. Normally, it didn't get above the low seventies in the summer, but today was T-shirt-and-shorts weather, and there were more people than usual on the beach. Flying kites and having picnics, walking solo or in pairs along the sand. Dogs of all shapes and sizes ran joyously though the water, their tongues lolling out and their barks carrying on the sea breeze.

But Summer's favorite part of the day so far had been running into Poppy and her boyfriend on the beach. They'd been walking hand in hand, looking very much in love when Summer had spotted them. Poppy had run up to hug her, then breathlessly introduced Justin to her and Angie. It had felt like they were all old friends, a feeling that was so precious to Summer, that she wanted to tuck it away. To protect it deep inside her heart. This was what she'd been hoping for when she'd moved to Christmas Bay. This sense of belonging.

She fell into step beside Angie again, loving how the sun felt on her bare shoulders. It was such a beautiful day, and she'd been having such a good time, that she'd almost forgotten about the letter from Eric. Almost.

Angie looked over with a frown. "You got quiet all of a sudden. What's wrong?"

"Just thinking."

"About Beau?"

She'd just finished telling Angie about their coffee date, which was tomorrow. Something that she was nervous about despite trying to convince herself it was just business.

"No. Actually, something else. Surprisingly, since I haven't been able to stop thinking about Beau since he came out to my place the other day. I'm so confused. I honestly don't know which way is up."

Angie slowed, her sleek brown hair blowing around her face. She looked worried, and that made Summer worried. Was there such a thing as just business with Beau? Was she prepared to let him back into her life? She thought she'd made the right decision the day she'd left Earl's Antiques, but now, here she was again. Pulled right back into his orbit. But that was Beau for you. He was hard to quit.

"He hurt you," Angie said. "It's no wonder you're confused. You're still not over him."

Summer sighed, digging into the sand with her toes. "Is it that obvious?"

"It's okay, you know. You loved him. These things take time."

"But ten years? That seems excessive."

"You're a romantic."

"I'm a schmuck."

Angie laughed. "You are not."

"Oh, I beg to differ. He has this way of looking at me. He used to look at me like that all the time. He *still* looks at me like that, and I don't know if he means to, or if it means anything at all, but it literally melts me. It melts my insides. Tell me again how smart it is to be doing business with this man?"

Smiling, Angie looked out over the water. "I think it's sweet."

"You said he was an ass."

"He is. But he's not over you, either, Summer. You can count on that."

Could she? She didn't really know. But if she wasn't over him, and there was a chance he wasn't over her, how was any of this going to end well? The answer was, it wasn't. It wasn't going to end well at all.

"So," Angie said, "if you weren't thinking about him just now, what were you thinking about?"

Summer bit the inside of her cheek. She hadn't told her friend about the letter yet. And she hadn't told her about the things that had been leading up to it these last few weeks, either. Mostly because she'd been in denial. The dark SUV that kept driving by French Vanilla wasn't really anything to be worried about. The prickly feeling at the back of her neck was just her imagination. She was reading into things, being dramatic. That's what she'd kept telling herself. Until she'd gotten the letter.

At the thought of it now, her stomach twisted. It was typewritten and wasn't signed, but it said things only Eric would know. And now he knew where she *lived.* She thought she'd been so careful when she'd left Eugene, but looking back, she probably hadn't covered her tracks as well as she could have. A few close friends had known, and it would only take one of them to slip up.

She came to a stop and touched her toe to a pretty pink shell in the sand. Angie stopped, too.

"Summer..."

"Yeah?"

"What's going on? Really."

Summer looked over and managed a smile. But her friend knew her too well to be fooled by it.

"Eric is back," she said.

"Eric..." Angie repeated, as if she wasn't quite sure what Summer meant. And then her brows shot up. *"Eric?"*

Summer nodded.

"When? *How?*"

Angie was one of the only people Summer had confided in about her experience in Eugene. She didn't like talking about it because she always felt paranoid afterward. Eric had been so clever, never quite leaving proof of anything, and always easing up before she decided to go to the police. So there was no real record of the things he'd done. It was her word against his.

"He left a letter in my mailbox the other day."

Angie stared at her. "What did it say?"

"Just that he misses me, he wishes we could be friends again, blah, blah, blah. It wasn't threatening or anything. It was perfectly polite, as usual. So if I showed it to anyone, they'd think I was the one off my rocker."

"Oh, Summer. I'm so sorry. How long has it been since you've heard from him?"

"A few years. But I've been feeling weird lately. I've

just had this feeling, like I'm being watched or something. It's creepy."

Angie crossed her arms over her chest like she was suddenly cold. "So he's back, after all this time. Do you think he *lives* here?"

"I doubt it, or I probably would've run into him by now. He's probably taking weekend jaunts over here."

"The whole thing is just so *weird.* You guys didn't even date, did you?"

"No, but he did ask me out and I said no. We were friends, though, before he started getting jealous. He didn't like if I went out with other guys or did anything without him. And then it just went downhill from there."

Summer shivered thinking about it. That had been a low point. She'd felt isolated in Eugene. She'd missed her parents, who'd moved away by that time, and her sister, who'd been starting a new life in Washington. But the person she'd missed most of all was Beau. He'd always been there for her, and understood her so well. She'd felt safe with him—something that she longed for. Especially when Eric had started rattling her.

"You need to go to the police, Summer."

"I know. I know I do, but it was such a bad experience last time. I don't think they believed me at all. And I really don't have any proof, except for this letter, and it looks like it could be written by my great-aunt."

"You still need to go. You have to start documenting this stuff in case you need to get a restraining order. He could be dangerous."

Summer nodded.

"Do you want me to go with you?" Angie asked.

"No, it's okay." Word traveled so fast in Christmas

Bay that she wasn't looking forward to showing up at the department at all. But if she had to go, she wanted to handle it alone. As inconspicuously as possible. And that meant by herself, at least for now. "Thank you, though."

"Promise you'll go?"

"I promise."

Angie shook her head and began walking again, her hands in her jeans' pockets. "I wonder why he showed up again. What triggered it?"

Summer walked slowly beside her friend, looking down at the imprints her feet were making in the sand. A tiny crab scurried sideways toward the water and then disappeared in the next frothy wave. She wondered what had triggered Eric's reappearance, too. What spark had lit inside his mind to make him fixate on her again after all this time? There had to be a reason why. *Something...*

Frowning, she looked out over the water. And then it hit her. She stopped. Angie stopped, too.

"I know why he's here," she said, the wind whipping at her ponytail.

"Why?" Angie asked.

"Of course. Of *course.* It makes sense."

Angie reached for her hand. Her friend's fingers were cold.

"Summer?"

"My birthday," she managed. "He's here because of my birthday."

Beau stood in the greeting card section of Cartwrights staring down at the selection of birthday cards. Summer's birthday was on July Fourth, a hard birthday to forget. Every year since their breakup, he thought about her on Independence Day. Wondered how she was doing and trying to convince himself that he was better off without her. Lately, that wasn't going so hot.

"Whose birthday is it?" Mary asked behind him. He'd sent her off to get some potato chips to go with the hot dogs they were grilling tonight, and he thought she'd be occupied for longer.

"Nobody's."

"Hmm." She stepped close and looked up at him skeptically.

"Hmm, what?"

"It's just weird that you'd be looking at birthday cards, if it's nobody's birthday."

This kid was too much.

"Did you get chips?" he asked.

"Yeah. And some treats for Roo, is that okay?"

He glanced down at the things she had in the cart. Sure enough, there were several kinds of dog treats and a tennis ball toy with a rope attached. This was the most spoiled dog in the history of dogs.

"You know she shreds those things," he said, nodding to the tennis ball. "It'll probably last five minutes."

"I know, but she loves balls."

He smiled. "Okay. Balls it is."

"So...whose birthday is it, Uncle Beau?"

She wasn't going to let this go. He should've sent her to get the hot dogs, too.

"Mary..."

"You don't have to tell me."

"But you're going to bug me about it until I do."

"Yeah. Probably."

"Summer's birthday is coming up in July."

"Then why are you looking at the cheesy cards? Why aren't you looking at the good cards?"

He didn't even know what to say to that. Plus, were these cheesy?

Mary took him by the hand and tugged him a few feet over.

"Here," she said. "These are the nice ones. The blank ones are the best. That way you can write what you want in them."

He had absolutely no idea what he would write. If he even bought one, that is. Would giving her a birthday card be weird? Would *not* giving her one be weird? Or should he do something more, like flowers or something? It was a big birthday, after all, and she loved those. Correction, she used to love those. He didn't know what she thought about them anymore.

He frowned, looking down at the cards. There were so *many.*

Mary sighed dramatically. "Do you want me to help you?"

"I don't need any help."

She stared up at him.

"Okay," he said. "I need some help."

"This one is pretty. It has butterflies. Does she like butterflies?"

"I have no idea."

"Does she like sparkles?"

"Um…"

"Everyone likes sparkles." Mary pulled one of the cards from the shelf and it was, indeed, sparkly. Beau's gut tightened. He wasn't a sparkly kind of guy. This was probably a mistake.

Mary tossed it in the cart, sensing his hesitation. "Chillax, Uncle Beau. We can put it back if you change your mind."

He might not chillax, but he was definitely going to change his mind. The only reason he was still standing there was to pacify his niece. At least, that's what he told himself as she pulled another card from the shelf. This one was simpler, and it had a mountain stream on the front. With a guy fishing in it.

"This one!" Mary said.

"Okay," he said. "Toss it in."

She did and smiled up at him. "You like her, right?"

"No."

"She's pretty," Mary said. "And nice. *I* like her."

"She is pretty. And nice. But I don't like her, not like that."

"Mom says you do. So does Aunt Poppy."

"Whatever," he mumbled.

"Mom says you're just scared."

He made a mental note to tell Cora to zip it about his love life. Or lack thereof. At least in front of Mary.

"*Are* you scared?" Mary asked.

"Me? No. I'm not scared." That was a lie. Deep down, he knew he was. But that wasn't something he planned on admitting to anyone. Especially to his sweet niece who, at the moment, was looking at him with more than a little curiosity.

"So you don't ever...like, want to have a girlfriend again? Or get married?"

He stared down at her.

"It's okay if you don't want to get married," Mary

said. "Mom says she's never going to get married again. Not after Dad."

Beau frowned and put a hand on Mary's thin shoulder. She suddenly looked close to crying. Her big, blue eyes were glassy. He hoped she wouldn't. He hated it when she cried; it was gut-wrenching.

Max had been a good father to her. Technically, he'd been her stepfather, but Mary had adored him and had never shown any interest in meeting her birth father, who'd been Cora's first love in high school. But Beau wondered what might happen now. Now that she was grieving this monumental loss. Curiosity might get the best of her.

"I know you and your mom miss your dad very much," Beau said. "I'm sorry, Mary. He was so proud of you."

She sniffed and gave him a small smile. It looked like the threat of tears had passed, but the anguished expression on her freckled face remained.

"Do you think he'd be sad if Mom got married again?"

Beau pulled her into a hug. "I think he'd want her to be happy," he said into her soft hair. "And he'd want you to be happy, and if her getting married again someday would make you both happy, then there you have it. But that's a long way off, kiddo. Right now you just have to heal, and that takes time."

Mary nodded, pulling away again. "I know. But I worry about my mom. She misses him and she's lonely. I can hear her crying sometimes. She doesn't know I can, but I do."

Beau's heart twisted. Cora was such a strong person that sometimes he forgot how much she must be struggling. He made a vow to check in on her more often. To make sure she knew how much she was loved. He didn't say it enough. Hell, he really didn't say it at all—he always just assumed that his cousins knew how he felt about them.

"I think if you like Summer," Mary said, "you should tell her. You could just write in in the card, and you wouldn't even have to say it out loud."

"Why do you think I like her?"

"I don't know." She shrugged. "I just do. I can kind of tell."

Beau considered this. Was he putting out some kind of subconscious vibe? Probably.

"Thanks for the advice," he said. "I'll think about it, okay?"

"Okay."

"Should we go get the hot dogs now? And stuff to make s'mores for dessert?"

Mary broke into a grin. "Yeah."

"Okay, kid. Let's go."

He turned the shopping cart with one hand, its old wheels squeaking, and put his other arm around Mary. His shoulder ached, the pain radiating down his biceps and into his elbow. But it was funny—it wasn't nearly as noticeable when it was resting like this on Mary. Ironic, he guessed.

Maybe he should try leaning on people more often.

Summer sat on an upside-down feed bucket beside Tank's pasture and answered the FaceTime call from her mom. The afternoon sun felt good after the chill of the morning. But what warmed her most was the sight of her mom's sunburned face when it popped up on the screen.

Summer smiled. It had been a while since they'd talked. Her parents had been on a cruise for the last two weeks, but were headed home to Arizona and its warm, dry climate that provided relief for her dad's arthritis.

"Hi, honey!" her mom said. People with suitcases and backpacks were bustling around her and it was obvious she was calling from their gate at the airport.

"Hey, Mom."

"Your father went to get us a sandwich, but he said to tell you hi and that he loves you. Is it warm there? You're outside?"

Summer panned the phone briefly over Tank, who was sunbathing in a patch of dirt a few feet away. "It's really warm," she said, looking into the phone again. "It's a pretty day here."

"I can see that. My grandgoat looks fat and happy. We miss you."

"I miss you, too. How was the cruise?"

"It was good. Long. Probably too long. I miss Yogi, he probably won't even remember us."

Yogi was their chubby black cat, who most certainly *would* remember them but might be miffed enough not to show it. He had a habit of pooping in her dad's shoes when they went on vacation, something that Summer found endlessly funny. Her dad, not so much.

"He'll be fine," she said. "Your pet sitter sounds amazing."

"She is. And I just booked her for our trip to see you for your big day. Our girl is going to be thirty, I can hardly believe it."

Her father appeared behind her mom and leaned over her shoulder with a wide smile. He was sunburned, too.

"Hey, doll. What gives?"

"Hey, Dad."

"I was just telling Summer we can't wait to see her for her birthday."

At the mention of her birthday, Summer's stomach dropped. Everyone who knew her, knew how much she loved celebrating her birthday. It was a favorite tradition held over from her childhood. She loved the cake, and the cards, and the *love*. She adored it all, really. She'd only had one birthday with Beau, but he'd done it right. He'd taken her to dinner and had given her a lovely solitaire necklace that she still wore to this day. She'd actually been wearing it the day she'd walked into Earl's Antiques to see him standing at the cash register, painfully handsome and just as distant as ever.

But that wasn't the reason her stomach was upside down now. That had everything to do with Eric. She'd put two and two together yesterday and since then she'd felt like his reappearance in her life was even more ominous. They'd been close once, and he knew exactly how she felt about her birthdays, especially the milestone ones. For whatever reason, he'd decided he wasn't going to miss her thirtieth.

The thought sent chills into her scalp.

"Honey?" her mom said, leaning closer to the screen. "What's wrong?"

Summer shook her head quickly. Her parents would only worry if she told them and there wasn't anything they could do about it anyway.

"Nothing," she said.

Her mom looked skeptical. But got distracted when Summer's dad tapped her on the shoulder and handed her a sandwich in a brown paper bag.

"How's the business going?" her dad asked. "Last time we talked, you said you were going to canvass places in Christmas Bay. How did that go?"

She wasn't super excited about telling them about Beau, but if she might be working with him, they'd find out soon enough anyway. Especially when they came to visit.

Swallowing hard, she leaned forward on the bucket, feeling its sharp edges bite into her rear end. "Well, you're not going to guess who I ran into..."

Her mother's eyebrows rose as she bit into her sandwich.

"Beau Evers," she finished evenly.

Her dad stared into the screen. Her mom put her sandwich down and dabbed at her lips with a napkin, looking like she was trying to choose her words carefully.

"Beau?" her dad said. "Your Beau?"

"Well, he's not *my* Beau. But yeah."

"Oh," her mom said. "Well. How's he doing? Is he still fishing?"

She said this with a tone. Summer's parents had nursed her back to life after Beau had broken up with her. They'd known exactly how in love with him she'd been, and exactly how hurt she'd been when he'd walked away. When it came to Beau, there was no love lost there.

"He's okay," she said. "It's a long story, but he's in Christmas Bay to help run his grandpa's antique shop for a while. Earl passed away in the spring."

"Oh, I'm sorry to hear that," her dad said. "So he's not fishing?"

"He's not. He's got a shoulder injury."

"Hmm." Her mom bit into her sandwich again. It was hard to tell what she was thinking, but Summer could guess well enough. She was fiercely protective of her daughters. Some choice words were probably going through her head right about then.

"Anyway," Summer went on, "he's the furniture buyer for the antique shop and we're talking about working together. This could be really good for my business. They've got a great reputation up and down the coast, and people come from all over to shop there."

Her dad gave her mom a quick look.

"Don't worry," she said. "It's only business."

"You're a big girl, Summer," her mom said. "But we're always going to worry about you. We just want you to be careful, that's all. Even if this is just business, be careful."

She nodded. The warning was valid. She thought about her coffee date with Beau the next day and wondered how that would go. And then wondered how long she'd be able to keep her protective wall up where he was concerned. There was something about him—there'd always been something about him—that chipped away at her defenses. He was her kryptonite.

"We're getting ready to board, honey," her dad said. "We'll call when we land, okay?"

"Be safe, have a good flight."

Her mom smiled. "We love you."

"Love you, too."

She hung up and stared out over Tank's pasture, lost

in thought. After a minute, her gaze shifted to her goat, who was still lying in the exact same position as when she'd sat down to answer the phone. The sun had gone behind a cloud a few minutes ago and she shivered, watching him. He actually hadn't moved a muscle since she'd been there and, now that she thought about it, he hadn't run to meet her like he normally did when she came out in the mornings.

She stood, brushing the seat of her jeans off. "Tank?"

He lay there, his stomach moving up and down. But he didn't raise his head.

"Tank?"

She walked over to the fence, worried now. Her heart beat heavily against her breastbone.

Opening the gate, she stepped inside, her boots sinking into the soft, moist dirt. And, still, Tank didn't move. She walked quickly over and knelt down beside him, resting a hand on his neck. His eyes rolled as he looked up at her.

"Oh, buddy." Her belly sank. He was sick.

She pulled her phone from her back pocket and dialed her vet's number.

Hoping against hope that it wasn't as serious as it looked.

Chapter Six

Beau sat in a corner booth at the little café and looked at his watch again. She was late. But he didn't want to rush her by texting so soon.

Rubbing his jaw, he sat back and watched a few women push the door open from the outside, their hair flying everywhere from the ever-present coastal wind. Maybe something had come up and she was on her way. Or maybe she'd decided to stand him up, and if that was the case, he guessed it would serve him right. For treating her the way he had in college. For breaking her heart and expecting her to be open to any kind of relationship with him again, even if it was only the working kind.

He took a sip of his coffee and set it down again, licking the bitterness from his lips. He'd wait another few minutes and then he'd text. Or maybe he'd call. He wanted to make sure she was okay. His mind, as usual, went to those worst-case scenarios. He guessed he'd always be a little overprotective when it came to the people he cared about.

Sitting back against the booth, he stared out the window to the cars passing on Main Street. *People he cared about...* The thought had materialized before he could help it. Before he could analyze it and properly tuck it back where it had come from. Or better yet, get rid of it altogether. But he'd acknowledged the notion now, so it was too late.

He shifted in the booth, suddenly uncomfortable. He guessed he shouldn't be surprised by the fact that he'd lumped Summer into a group of people he cared about. Maybe even loved. If he was honest with himself, he might say he'd never stopped loving her. But that wasn't a thought he cared to entertain for long because it made him feel mildly terrified. Because if he'd never stopped loving her, he'd have to admit that he loved her still, and that was just too much to process. At least without a stronger drink in his hand.

He looked at his watch again. Twenty minutes late now. Summer might still be mad at him, but she wasn't the type to stand him up like this. She was too nice for that. She should've called by now.

He fished his phone out of his pocket, his shoulder screaming in protest as usual, and pulled her number up to text her.

Hey, just making sure I'm at the right place? The Espresso Bean on Main?

Setting his phone down on the table, he stared at the screen. The text went through okay. He kept watching for it to be read, because she had her read receipts on, something he'd noticed the other day. But nothing. His gut tightened. Just because she hadn't gotten his text didn't mean anything was wrong. But at the same time, he couldn't shake the sudden feeling that something *was* wrong.

"Can I get you any more coffee?"

He looked up to see a blond, twentysomething server standing over him holding a coffeepot.

"Please."

"Are you Beau Evers?" she asked, filling his cup to the brim. The steam curled into the air, the scent reminding him of coming here with his grandfather when he was a kid. The café had changed owners a couple of times over the years, but they'd always served comfort food. Crispy grilled-cheese sandwiches. Rich clam chowder with saltines on the side. Coffee that tasted like home—because of the chipped mugs it was served in, and not because of any particular roast.

He smiled up at her, remembering that he was supposed to be getting back into the dating game. That had been the plan, at least. And then Summer had reappeared, blowing all his plans right out of the water. "I am."

"I fish," she said. "Lake fishing, mostly."

Her cheeks colored and he saw how pretty she was. But his thoughts lay, like they always seemed to, with Summer. Again, he wondered where she was and he shifted in his seat, restless.

"Oh yeah?"

"I'm a fan of yours. I've been following you since Oklahoma."

She didn't need to elaborate. That tournament had rounded out one of his best years ever. The height of his career. Right before he'd blown out his shoulder.

"Thanks," he said. "I appreciate that."

She moved on to the next booth but cast a quick glance back at him.

Normally, he'd enjoy the attention. Might even let it go to his head a little. But instead he looked at his watch again. He didn't like the feeling in his chest—like someone had wrapped a rope around it and was pulling.

He didn't like it at all.

Beau drove out to Summer's place with the window down, the salty breeze blowing through the car. He'd ended up texting her again and then calling twice. There'd been no answer, so he'd paid his bill at the café, and headed straight for the Subaru parked out front. She'd probably think he was off his nut for driving all the way out to her house. Or maybe she'd think he was still hung up on her, but at this point, he didn't really care. He just needed to make sure she was alright.

Leaning forward, he squinted at her little house up ahead. Her old blue pickup was parked out front, standing sentry next to the shop. Which made this even more strange. She was home… Was she sick? Hurt? The thought made the hairs on his arms prickle.

Flipping on his blinker, he slowed and turned the Subaru onto her dirt drive. The gravel crunched underneath the all-terrain tires and the breeze coming through the window brought with it a few drops of the rain forecasted for earlier in the day.

Beau rolled the window up as he pulled alongside Summer's truck and came to a stop. He let the car idle for a few seconds while he looked around her property. Nothing seemed out of the ordinary, but his skin prickled just the same.

He turned the engine off and stepped out, breathing in the smell of the countryside. Then took her porch steps two at a time. The front door was open, with only a weathered screen door serving as a barrier to the inside. He knocked on its rickety wood frame. "Summer?"

No answer. No movement from inside at all.

"Summer?" he called again, this time louder.

He waited, the heaviness in his gut feeling more and more like a cinder block by the minute.

Reaching out, he grabbed the handle of the screen door but stopped short of yanking it open when he heard his name called behind him.

"Beau! I'm back here! In Tank's shed!"

He turned and jogged down the steps and over to the small pasture where the gate was swung open. The rustic red shed, open at one end with an overhang for shade on warm days, was to his right. He came around the side of it, relieved that she was there but knowing something was definitely wrong.

"Beau?"

Looking down, he saw her sitting in a bed of straw, the big, brown goat's head resting in her lap. Her hair was wild around her face, which was pale, almost ghostly looking. Dark smudges sat below her eyes and her lips were chapped and without color. It was the roughest he'd ever seen her look, and he'd once nursed her when she'd had a nasty case of bronchitis.

"Summer?" he bit out. "What's going on?"

As he said it, his gaze shifted to the goat, who was lying on his side, his breathing labored.

"The vet just left," she said. "He's been out twice so far."

As he got closer, he could see the smudges below her eyes was her mascara. She'd been crying.

He knelt down to one knee, the straw poking into his jeans. "What's wrong with him?"

"Acidosis," she said. Her voice sounded hoarse. Like she might not have slept at all. "It's when they eat too much grain."

He ran his hand down Tank's warm neck and the goat briefly closed his caramel-colored eyes.

"Is he going to be okay?" Beau asked.

"I think so. Dr. Poet thinks we caught it early, and he gave him some fluids and some antibiotics that should keep him from getting a secondary infection. Now, we just wait. He's so weak, though." Her eyes filled with quick tears and she looked away.

"Hey," he said. "Are you okay?"

She nodded. "I'm usually so careful with his food. Especially with his grain, because he's such a pig when it comes to grain, and I knew this could happen. But he got into the bag, and..."

She sniffed and touched her nose with the back of her hand.

"It was an accident," he said. "It could've happened to anyone."

"But that's the thing, I'm not sure it was an accident."

He frowned. Watching the way her chin quivered and feeling that to his very core.

"What do you mean?"

She shifted in the straw, causing Tank to reposition himself, too. With a deep groan, the goat moved onto his other side and then tucked his knobby knees underneath him. With his head raised like this, he looked more alert now, much less dire than when Beau had walked up on them a minute ago.

Summer must've thought so, too, because she smiled and gave him a gentle scratch behind one floppy ear.

"The fluids probably made him feel better," she said.

"Summer."

She looked over at him, her eyes bloodshot.

"What do you mean it wasn't an accident?"

She took a deep breath, her breasts rising and falling underneath her worn University of Oregon T-shirt. There was a faint outline of a lacy bra through the thin white cotton.

"Remember that letter I told you about the other day?" she said. "The one from my old coworker?"

"Yeah. Want to talk about it now?"

"I think I need to. I need to tell someone what's going on. Angie knows, but she doesn't live here, and if something else happens…"

"Something else." He didn't like how that sounded. "What do you mean 'something else'?"

Summer had been gazing over at Tank, but at this, she let her eyes shift to Beau again. Her pupils were big black orbs, as if simply mentioning the letter had given her a shot of adrenaline.

"I'm starting to think the guy who sent it could be dangerous."

She looked down at Tank again and patted his side. He stretched out with a soft groan, closed his eyes and started snoring like a dog.

Summer got up and brushed the straw off her jeans. "I think he'll be okay for a little while. Do you want to come inside for some coffee? I'm so sorry I forgot about meeting you this morning. I haven't checked my phone, I'm sure you called."

"Don't worry about that. If you think he'll be alright, coffee sounds good. You could probably use a breather."

She brushed her hair away from her face. "I'll clean up. I'm a mess."

"You look beautiful." As soon as he said it, he felt his neck heat. It was true. She was beautiful. Messy hair, running mascara and all. But Beau wasn't in the habit of letting things like that slip. The last thing he needed right now was Summer knowing how he really felt. But that also begged the question, How *did* he feel? The answer was complicated and not necessarily something he wanted to explore with her standing so close that he could smell her light, flowery scent. So, as per usual, he pushed it away to deal with later. Or not deal with later.

With one more look at Tank, Summer walked out the gate and Beau followed, latching it behind him. It was starting to rain in earnest now, and the temperature had dropped enough that he wished he'd brought a jacket. The weather on the coast was always mercurial, changing at the drop of a hat, and it surprised him how quickly he'd forgotten that. His mother used to dress him in layers, his dad always teasing her about it because Beau would show up at school looking like the Stay Puft Marshmallow Man. That was long before his parents' marriage had fallen apart and a bitter seed had been planted in his heart.

Now, he could hardly believe there'd ever been a time when he'd thought relationships would work just because there was love involved. That people would stick around and promises would be kept just because they were made.

He used to think he'd be the kind of person to break the cycle his mom and dad had set in motion, not perpetuate it. But he'd done the same thing to Summer—he'd left. He'd broken promises, too. It made him sad to think about it, so he made it a rule not to. Only, sometimes, the memory hit him just right, out of the blue, like now. On an ordinary summer day, with raindrops stinging his face and the scent of a woman he'd left long ago filling his senses.

Summer walked up the porch steps, holding her hair back with one hand. She turned and smiled at him over her shoulder, and that smile did something to his insides. Where he was the coldest. It warmed him some, but he didn't smile back. He just walked up the steps after her, wishing suddenly that he'd never come there. He could've had someone else check on her. He could've kept his distance, but he hadn't, and now here he was. Feeling the resurrection of a love he'd told himself had died a long time ago.

She opened the screen door and he followed her inside. The house was small and, like the shop, the space was warm and cozy. It smelled good, like vanilla candles and woodsmoke. She had pictures of her family hanging on the walls and quilts draped over the overstuffed couch and chairs that looked handmade. The walls were painted a farmhouse white and there were red accents everywhere. Pillows, lampshades, flowerpots where healthy green ferns and fat succulents were hanging next to the living room windows.

"I'm just going to make a pot of coffee and change clothes really quick," Summer said. "Make yourself at home. Can I get you anything first?"

"Thanks, I'm good."

He watched her climb the stairs, the old hardwood creaking underneath her boots, before turning to look around. It was a sweet little house. But she was isolated out here. Her nearest neighbors were barely visible and she was surrounded on three sides by pastures and countryside. And beyond that, the blue horizon where you could see the ocean on a clear day. He thought about what she'd said about the guy who'd sent that letter. That he might be dangerous. He had no idea what that was about, but he was going to find out.

Putting his hands in his jeans' pockets, he walked over to a bookcase by the front door. It was old and had the distinct look of being refinished by a knowing hand. One of Summer's own pieces, no doubt. She had more photographs in frames lining the shelves and a mixture of classic and contemporary books, hardcover and soft. Knickknacks that looked like they had sentimental value, bookends that looked like antiques. And a vintage typewriter, a Royal, that he lightly ran his fingers over now, thinking of his grandpa and how much he would've appreciated this. He'd had lots of antique typewriters in his shop. And if his customers ever wanted one that he didn't have, he'd find it for them. He'd been so good at that, the treasure hunting thing.

The thought made Beau swallow hard. His grandpa had never met Summer, but he would've liked her, there was no doubt.

He let his gaze sweep the rest of the shelves. A small picture in a miniature frame caught his eye. He picked it up to see that it was of him and Summer, taken when they'd first started dating. It was grainy, out of focus, but the couple inside the tarnished silver frame had clearly been in love. She had her head in the crook of his neck and her eyes were closed. He was smiling. From something she'd said? From something he'd done? He couldn't remember exactly where it had been taken or who'd taken it. Probably at a college party or something. But she'd kept it. And, most importantly, she'd kept it out. Where she could see it every day. Where other people could see it, too.

He heard her coming down the stairs and he set the picture down, backing away from the bookshelf. Turning, he saw that she'd put on a pair of faded jeans and an oversized T-shirt. Her hair was twisted up in a bun and her face was scrubbed clean, her cheeks rosy, her freckles standing out on her nose.

When she saw what he'd been looking at, the smile on her lips wilted.

"Oh…uh…"

He nodded toward the photo. "I'd forgotten about that one."

"Yeah," she said quietly. "I've had it forever. Well, since we first got together. I always liked it."

"I'm surprised you didn't toss it when we broke up."

"Well. I did. But I fished it out of the garbage a few hours later."

He smiled. "You never could get rid of anything."

"I'm better at it now. But sentimental things…" Her voice trailed off.

The fact that this picture still meant something to her was enough to warm his blood. It was also enough to make him want to run away. What a familiar feeling *that* was. He was all kinds of screwed up. And she was all kinds of lovely standing there smelling so good. Suddenly, he had the urge to take her in his arms, to pull her close and nuzzle that hollow spot at the base of her throat. He had the urge to kiss her like he had when they'd been young and in love and hadn't worried about their future. Until that future had gotten closer and their love had taken on a life of its own.

They stood there watching each other, the thick silence settling between them. Finally, Beau looked away and rubbed the back of his neck. His shoulder ached with the movement, his arm protesting at being raised at such a sharp angle.

"The coffee is probably ready," Summer said. And he was glad she'd said something, so he wouldn't have to.

He followed her into the kitchen, which was also painted white. There were little bursts of color everywhere, which he now recognized as her trademark. Fuchsia dishtowels, a bright red teapot that looked like a giant tomato sitting on the stovetop, flower-print curtains that reminded him of an English garden. Oranges in a bowl on the counter, looking plump and juicy and ready to be peeled. He could smell their citrusy scent from where he stood, along with the dark scent of coffee.

He imagined Summer cooking in this kitchen. Eating dinner in the breakfast nook all by herself. It made him feel lonely for her, even though she seemed happy and confident and independent living alone. If he felt lonesome for anyone, it should probably be for himself. Before coming home to Christmas Bay, he'd drink protein shakes for dinner. Or would swing by and pick up takeout on the way to the lake, or the river, or wherever he was fishing at the time.

It was funny how, in just a few short weeks, his perspective had shifted. A few weeks ago, he wouldn't have thought twice about having dinner by himself. But now he had his cousins and his niece to come home to. They usually ate together, laughing and talking about their day, which mostly consisted of antique-shop things, but also included the start of middle school in the fall for Mary. That would be a big deal. There would be drama, boys, puppy love. Beau knew without anyone having to say it that she saw him as a father figure. He couldn't take the place of her dad, of course, but he was a comfort in his absence. It was all temporary. They all knew that, but he found he liked the thought.

He looked away from the breakfast nook and let his gaze settle on Summer as she poured coffee into two mismatched mugs. Again, the thought of her living alone nibbled at his consciousness, but this time it was more of a concern for her safety as her words from earlier reverberated through his head.

Might be dangerous...

Turning, she handed him his mug and then sat on a stool at the kitchen island. He did the same and took a sip of the steaming coffee.

"Okay," he said, setting his mug down. "Tell me about this letter you got. And tell me who wrote it."

She tapped her thumb against the handle of her mug, two worry lines forming between her brows.

"After I graduated from college," she said, "I got a job at a marketing firm in Eugene. I was part of the art department and I thought it was a perfect fit. I had a creative outlet and I was making good money. I liked my coworkers, my boss, all that. We got pretty tight, all of us."

He watched her, saw the way her knee had started bouncing under the bar. The way she kept stirring her coffee with her spoon, the stainless steel clanking rhythmically against the mug.

"A guy named Eric Malcom and I were especially close," she continued. "We were good friends, did a lot of things together outside of work. I think he had a crush on me. He asked me out at one point and I said no because we worked together, and he seemed to take that okay. Until he didn't."

Beau frowned. "Go on."

"He started acting possessive. A little weird. He'd ask where I was going and when I was going to be back when I was with other friends. He'd be manipulative when he felt like he wasn't getting enough attention. My first couple of birthdays at the firm were really fun, and it had become a tradition to celebrate it together. But when I began putting some distance between us, he didn't react well to that. Around the time of my last birthday at the firm, he started calling and texting more than usual. Leaving little notes and presents for me. It was creepy, but nothing anyone would necessarily think was strange. I finally reported it, but the police didn't take it seriously and neither did my supervisor at work. It was a mess, really. I started feeling unsafe just walking to my car at night. He never threatened me outright, but I was scared anyway. Scared enough that I finally quit and decided to move here."

He watched her. She was chewing the inside of her cheek now, her knee still bouncing underneath the bar.

"So you didn't come here just to restore furniture?"

"Kind of. I'd always wanted to. It was my dream to

eventually start my own business. Eric knew that. We'd talked about it a lot. The stuff with him just gave me the push I needed. So I quit and moved, but he didn't know anything about me relocating to Christmas Bay. I kept it quiet when I left, and I'm careful not to put my name out there on social media. I have pages for the business, but I use my middle name and I don't post pictures of myself. But in this day and age, I guess it wouldn't take much to track a person down if you really wanted to."

No, it wouldn't. But he didn't say that out loud. He didn't want to freak her out any more than she already was.

"So you think he sent that letter?" he asked.

She nodded.

"What did it say?"

"Same kind of stuff. Nothing overtly threatening, just that he missed me and was sad we aren't close anymore, things like that. It makes me feel paranoid even telling you this, because it sounds like I'm the one having a hard time moving on, not the other way around."

"I know you, Summer. If you think there's something wrong with this guy, then there's something wrong. You need to trust your instincts on this."

She gave him a small smile and, finally, her knee grew still underneath the counter. "Thank you for that. I guess I needed to hear it."

He waited a beat, waited for her to take another sip of her coffee, before leaning forward on one elbow. Close enough that he could see the flecks of caramel in her eyes.

"What about Tank?" he asked. "You think this guy might've had something to do with that?"

She frowned, the little worry lines between her brows reappearing. "The only thing I know for sure is that I have a bad feeling. I'm *very* careful about his food for exactly this reason. He gets into everything. It wouldn't take much for someone to research and figure out what could make a goat sick. And overeating isn't going to be something that anybody could prove was done maliciously. Poison? Yes. But not overeating. That bag of food was opened, but not by me. I use scissors, and it was torn. I never do that because it makes it harder to close afterwards."

He nodded, absorbing this. If her gut feeling was right, if this guy had made sure Tank ate enough grain to get sick, that made him a sociopath. And if he could do that to a poor animal, what would stop him from hurting a person? What would keep him from doing something to Summer?

Beau shifted on the stool, suddenly uncomfortable.

"Do you think I'm overreacting?" she asked. "I know it's a big jump from texts and letters to actually hurting Tank."

"Was the letter postmarked? Did he send it in the mail or do you think he was actually here? In Christmas Bay?"

"It wasn't postmarked. No stamp. He was here." She shook her head. "I've been seeing a strange SUV at the coffee stand where I work. On the weekends, mostly. And always at night, when I can't make out who's driving. But I just thought..." Her voice trailed off and she shrugged. But the stress on her face was clearly visible.

"You need to go to the police," he said. "Don't wait."

"I know. I will. Angie said the same thing when I saw her last. I promised I would."

"Good," he said. "You can call now and I'll stay with you until they come." The fact was, Summer was mostly alone here. Her family lived out of state and she was dealing with something potentially serious. She needed support.

"I can't ask you to do that."

"You're not asking. And I want to."

She looked down at her coffee cup and nodded. "Okay. I'd actually love the company. I think I'm more shaken by this than I want to admit."

"Of course you are."

She looked so lovely right then, so completely vulnerable, that the urge to pull her close washed over him again. His hands actually itched with the desire to hold her and touch her. How long had it been since he'd held Summer in his arms? A decade? Yet he could remember the feel of her, the softness and warmth of her body against his, so well. Some things didn't fade with time—they only intensified. And his desire for Summer was one of those things.

They looked at each other. Sitting there with the rain tapping against the kitchen windowpanes. Since Summer had reappeared a few weeks ago, there'd been plenty of times when the expression in her eyes had made him want to look away. And maybe that was because he could see himself reflected in them and he didn't like what he saw. Someone who'd been so callous all those years ago. Someone who, despite feeling regret about walking away from her, had refused to look back, and worse, had refused to acknowledge that regret at all. Was that the kind of man he was?

He thought of his grandfather and was ashamed. Would he be proud of Beau today? Or would he see someone who'd taken the easy way out?

Summer reached over and touched his hand. Her skin was like a shock of electricity, bringing him back to the moment.

"Where did you go?" she asked.

"Just thinking," he said. "About my grandpa."

"Feel like telling me about it?"

Beau sighed. "I just miss him."

"I know you do. I know how much you loved him."

He rubbed his jaw. He hadn't shaved that morning and there was scruff there. "I did, but it was more than that. He was like a second father to me. When my own dad wasn't around, he was always there. And now… sometimes it just hits out of nowhere. The fact that he's gone. I still have things to say to him, things I want him to know. Things I wanted him to see me do."

It was more than he was used to sharing. Even with his cousins. At least, not without a stiff drink first. But there was something about Summer that put him at ease. The kind of ease that he hadn't felt since college.

"What kinds of things?" she asked.

"The sportfishing, mostly. I wanted him to see the arc of my career. He was proud of that."

"He was proud of you, Beau," she said. "The fishing was just a bonus."

Beau wanted that to be true. And, mostly, he thought it was. But there were definitely things his grandpa had been disappointed in. Letting Summer go had been one of them. He'd known Beau had been in love and he'd known Summer had loved him back. When he'd found out that Beau had severed the relationship for the sake of his career, he'd thought it had had more to do with his inability to commit than the fishing itself. He'd told him so on more than one occasion. He hadn't wanted his grandson to throw away a chance at real happiness, and that's exactly what he'd done.

Beau shifted again, struggling with the memory. He wondered what Summer would think if she knew any of this. Of course, she had no clue that he might regret a damn thing. He could barely admit it to himself. And on most days couldn't even do that. But sitting there with her now, in her home, with the memory of her touch still lingering on his skin, something was forcing him to take a closer look. At his regrets. At his fears.

His gaze found hers again, where it seemed destined to be. She'd asked what kinds of things he'd wanted his grandfather to know. Maybe she was asking because she was being nice. Or maybe she really wanted to know.

"I'm afraid I'm never going to be able to fish professionally again," he said.

Chapter Seven

Summer knew the words, spoken so evenly, had been hard for Beau to say.

Without thinking about it, she placed her hand gently over his. And instead of him moving away, like she'd half expected him to, he remained still, his skin warm and rough underneath her fingertips. She felt the stiff little hairs on the back of his hand, the veins snaking over bone, the calluses on the sides of his pointer finger. From hours and hours and years and years of being on rivers and lakes with a fishing pole in his grip.

He looked up and she could see naked emotion in his eyes. She wasn't sure why he'd decided to confess this now, and to her of all people. Even when they'd been dating, he'd had a tendency to keep things close to his chest, to not share too much if it meant he had to open up to do it. Those moments had been few and far between, and she'd cherished each and every one because she'd fallen deeper in love with him when he let her in.

The feeling was strangely similar now and when she realized that her heart had started beating faster, she squeezed his hand and then let go. She leaned back, reminding herself that she needed to be wary where Beau was concerned. She couldn't allow herself to feel these emotions again. The ones that had swept her right off her feet and changed her life in ways she was still sorting through to this day. She'd once believed in true love. But in order to survive the breakup with Beau, a man she'd hoped to marry, she'd had to change how she looked at the world. She saw things differently now. She was more careful with her heart, slower to trust. And she really wasn't sure she believed in happily-ever-afters anymore. At least not the ones she'd loved to read about when she was a starry-eyed teenager.

She licked her lips and tried for some composure. "You'll fish again," she said. "You will."

"I don't know."

She wasn't sure what to say to that. But had the feeling she didn't need to say anything at all. He might just need to talk and have someone listen. She'd always been a good listener. It was one of the things that she and Eric had bonded over. At the thought of Eric, she was glad that Beau was sitting right there, close to her, making her feel safe.

"I've thought about this so many times," he said. "I've gone over it and over it, and the thought of not fishing professionally..." He looked across the kitchen. The rain was coming down harder now, streaming in miniature rivers down the foggy windows. "I've spent my entire adulthood chasing this. I've sacrificed a different kind of life in order to be good at it. Because, to be good, you *have* to sacrifice. You have to put in the hours and the weekends and the holidays. Even when you're tired, or sick, or just over it."

He wasn't saying it outright, but she wondered if he

was talking about their relationship. She remembered them fighting about it, and that word had come up repeatedly. *Sacrifice.* She'd hated feeling like she'd come second in his life. She'd always felt if he'd really loved her, fishing would've been the thing to go and not the other way around. Had it been fair of her to expect him to give it up? No, but she'd also never *asked* him to. She'd simply wanted him to want her as much as his other dreams.

He let his gaze settle on her again. "You're probably the last person who wants to sit here and listen to this."

"What do you mean?"

"I mean I know how you felt about the fishing. About all of it. And now I'm whining to you about the thought of losing it. Not very cool, I guess."

She smiled. "You don't know me very well then."

"I feel like I know you pretty well."

"Not if you think I wouldn't be here for a friend who's facing something like this."

He watched her, his jaw working. "Is that what we are? Friends?"

It was a good question. One that she hadn't considered until right then. The truth was they'd started out as friends. It made sense that they'd end up that way. And, yes, maybe they'd taken the long way around, but still. Here they were, talking over coffee about something important, and she'd even held his hand at one point. So, yeah. Friends for sure.

"Maybe we haven't kept in touch and sent Christmas cards," she said. "But you're always going to be somebody that I care about, Beau. Always."

He nodded, and looked down at his coffee. It was obvious he wasn't sure what to say, and that was okay. She was still letting it settle herself.

After a long moment, he pulled his phone from his back pocket. "I think you need to call the police now. No time like the present."

She'd almost forgotten about poor Tank, and the reality of the morning came rushing back. All of a sudden, she felt slightly sick to her stomach.

Swallowing hard, she took his phone and dialed the number.

Ben Martinez sat on the edge of Summer's love seat and jotted something down in a small notebook. He looked sharp in his dark uniform, his badge glinting in the early afternoon sunlight coming through the window. He was such a nice guy, so warm and pleasant, that if it wasn't for the uniform, she might've forgotten he was Christmas Bay's chief of police altogether.

She shifted on the couch, where Beau sat next to her. Just like he'd promised earlier, he'd stayed until Ben had arrived. For moral support, he'd told her with a reassuring smile. She was glad he was there. More than glad, really. His presence was making this whole thing a little easier to bear.

After a few seconds, Chief Martinez looked up. "Anything else you can remember? Any details you might've left out?"

She shook her head. "Not that I can think of."

"Well, if you remember something, just give me a call. It doesn't matter how small you think it is, with a case like this, it's all about establishing a pattern."

She exhaled slowly. This experience was already so

different from when she'd reported Eric in Eugene that she wanted to cry with relief. Ben believed her. Even if there wasn't a ton of evidence at the moment, he wasn't treating her like a paranoid person with too much time on her hands.

"In the meantime," he continued, "be diligent about locking your doors. I'm not saying he'll escalate to violence, but you never know with these things. It's much better to be too careful than not careful enough. I'd invest in some security cameras, too, and call us with anything suspicious. Please don't worry you'll be bothering us with something you might think is too small." He smiled. "That's our job."

Beau leaned forward, elbows on his knees, and clasped his hands together. "Do you think she's okay all the way out here, Chief? It's pretty far from town. How long would it take to respond to an emergency call?"

"That is a concern. As you know, we're a small department with limited manpower. Technically, it should only take about ten minutes, and we have the sheriff's office to assist if we need them to, but that's a best-case scenario. If you feel uncomfortable, you might consider staying in town for a few days and boarding your goat in a safe place. Just until things hopefully blow over. I know that's not ideal, but that's what I'd tell my own family if this was happening to them."

Summer nodded. She hated this. She didn't want to be chased away from her own home. And she didn't have unlimited funds for a motel, either. Boarding Tank? That would be even more expensive. But she knew the chief was right. This was her reality right now and she had to be smart about it. Better to spend some money changing her location for a few days than to end up hurt. Or worse.

She gave the chief a smile as he stood and tucked his notebook in his shirt pocket. Beau shook his hand and then watched him walk out the door.

She watched too. Wondering how this would all end. Wondering if she'd end up seeing Eric face to face.

Beau shrugged into his windbreaker as his physical therapist, a young woman fresh out of graduate school, typed something into her computer.

"So I'll see you next week?" she asked. "You're making real progress, Beau. I'm hopeful for this shoulder."

She'd said this before, yet it was only now that he was starting to believe her. Beau wasn't an optimist, but it was his instinct to grab onto hope wherever he could get it where sportfishing was concerned.

"I'll be here," he said.

"You just have to keep doing those exercises." She said this every time. He got the feeling a lot of people thought the exercises didn't work. "And be careful with any sudden movements. No walking your dog." She'd said this before, too. She didn't have anything to worry about there. He wasn't planning on walking Roo anytime soon.

"I won't."

She closed her laptop and pushed her tortoiseshell glasses up on her nose. "I've been meaning to ask, how's the sponsorship going? Are they being patient?"

He yanked the zipper up on his windbreaker and forced a smile. He'd known this question was coming and he'd dreaded it. Dreaded it because he didn't want to think about it. The fact was, his sponsor, a clothing line called Cast, wasn't going to wait for him forever. They'd been incredibly generous so far, but there was only so much they could do. If their guy wasn't fishing, what was there to sponsor?

"As patient as I can expect," he said. "But I'm not sure how long that'll last."

"I know you're anxious to get back out there. But we can't rush it. If you reinjure that joint, we're back to square one. Actually, it'll be worse than that..."

"I know."

She smiled. "I'm sorry. I'm nagging you, but I want this rehab to be successful."

"No worries. You're just doing your job. I'm going to be the best patient I can be."

"Good." She sighed, looking relieved that part of the conversation was over with. She probably got tired of having to sound like a broken record. "How's the antique shop? Every time I drive by, someone's coming in or out. It looks like you guys are doing a great business."

"We are. Cora and Poppy do all of the social media stuff, all of the marketing, and they're good at it, so I can't take any of the credit there. But I'm glad we're making a go of it."

"Earl would be glad, too. He was such a sweet man."

Beau was used to hearing this from people in town, but each time felt special. He was proud to be Earl Sawyer's grandson. Proud to be carrying on the family tradition at the shop, even though it had never been his plan. He wasn't sure what his cousins were going to do with it when he went back to fishing, *if* he went back to fishing, but they'd all done a pretty good job so far.

"Thank you," he said. "He was the best."

"Whenever I ran into him, he always gave me updates on your tournaments. Where you'd been and where you were going next. He sure was proud."

"He was the one who taught me how to fish," he said. "My dad wasn't around much, and I was getting into some trouble in school, fights and stuff, and he kind of thrust it on me. Turned out to be the best thing that ever happened to me."

"You're a natural."

"I don't know about that, but it's my life."

As soon as he said it, he realized how that sounded. Fishing was his life? It should be a passion, a career, and he should love it, no doubt, but his *life*? There was something fundamentally wrong with that, and he wasn't sure how to fix it. Or if he was in too deep to fix it at all.

His therapist walked him through the clinic and into the waiting area. He nodded to her then looked over at the young receptionist at the front desk—the one he'd been planning on asking out. She smiled and he smiled back. He thought briefly about following through and asking for her number. Imagined what picking her up for a date would be like and how the night would end. He thought about kissing her and putting his hands in her hair. And then, unsurprisingly, he thought about Summer.

He clenched his jaw and walked out the door.

"He's looking better," Dr. Poet said. He patted Tank on the rump while the goat was busy gobbling up a few alfalfa pellets from his bucket. "I think he got lucky this time."

Summer felt her shoulders relax for the first time since Dr. Poet, a tall man with impossibly curly hair and a kind smile, had pulled into her driveway. Tank seemed to have made a full recovery, but she'd been waiting for his follow-up exam to breathe easier. He *had* gotten lucky this time. But what if there was a next time? The thought sent chills up the back of her neck.

Standing, the vet picked up his bag. Most of his equipment was in his truck and he hadn't had to get any of it out this time. Which was good for her sweet goat. And good for her pocketbook, too. House calls were expensive.

"So," he said, his expression growing hard, "you said you think someone did this on purpose?"

"I don't have any proof, but yes. I've put a camera out here and above my front and back doors, but I'm still nervous. If someone wanted to hurt him again, they could."

"And you called the police?"

"I did. They said if I don't feel safe, I should find a way to stay in town for a while and board Tank."

Dr. Poet opened the gate for her then followed her through, latching it behind him. "Let's hope it doesn't come to that," he said. "But if it does, Rebecca and I could keep him at our place for a while. We've only got the chickens now, so there's plenty of room. You just say the word."

Her heart squeezed. She hadn't known him for long, just since she'd moved to town, but he'd always been so nice to her. He was a good man and a great vet. The best around really.

"Thank you," she said. "I appreciate that."

"The cameras are a good idea, I bet that'll take care

of the problem right there. Nobody wants their criminal activity recorded. Makes it pretty hard to deny any wrongdoing." He opened his truck door and tossed his bag inside. "I won't ask who you think this person is, but I'm sure you know that anyone who would hurt an animal wouldn't think twice about hurting a person. You be careful, Summer, you hear?"

He climbed into the driver's seat and closed the door. She leaned close to the open window. "I will, Dr. Poet, and thank you so much."

"Have a good afternoon."

"You too."

She stood there with her arms crossed over her chest and watched the truck make its way down her dirt drive, easing slowly over the few potholes that needed filling in. She had a busy day today. First the vet visit, then a delivery to Earl's Antiques. At the thought of seeing Beau again, butterflies tickled her ribcage. He'd been so sweet the other day, sitting with her until Chief Martinez had come. And then staying until he'd gone and making sure she didn't need anything else. She'd been unsettled before, but Tank getting sick had really shaken her.

Looking over at the enclosure, she was comforted by the way her goat was sunning himself. Not lying down in a worrisome way, but in that familiar happy way that she was so used to.

Nonetheless, as she turned and made her way to the shop, she wondered how long this particular peace was going to last.

Beau sat at his grandfather's desk in the back of the shop, sorting through some bills. Cora kept the books, but he'd gotten the mail today and had wanted to weed out the scrap before giving it to her. It was truly surprising how much junk mail they got. The only thing he snagged for the "keep" pile were some pizza coupons and a reminder from Roo's vet that her rabies shot was due.

"Uncle Beau!"

He looked up to see Mary roll in on her skates. She loved those damn things. Rolled around the shop in them constantly, delighting the customers and giving her mother a continuous headache. She had Roo on a short leash that was doubling as a pull rope.

Beau smiled. "You know you're not supposed to let her drag you around on your skates."

"I know, but it's fun. She likes it. It's like she's a sled dog or something."

"Or something."

"Summer just pulled up," Mary said, snapping her bubble gum. "Aunt Poppy says she's got the coffee table you asked for."

At the mention of Summer, Beau's gut tightened. He hadn't talked to her since going to check on her the other day, but he'd been thinking about her nonstop. Apparently, seeing more Summer just made him want more Summer. It was a fact that was getting harder and harder to ignore.

"Are you going to go out there like *that*?" Mary asked when he stood. She looked him up and down, making a face.

He glanced at himself. "Like what?"

"Like, all slouchy and stuff."

"Slouchy?"

"Like it's Saturday and you're watching a football game."

"What's wrong with what I wear to watch football?"

"It's slouchy."

He laughed. He was wearing jeans, a T-shirt and a baseball cap, but normally he wore collared sport shirts, so he guessed this was Mary's idea of slouchy. "I don't think I look *that* bad. And why does it matter anyway?"

She sighed, exasperated. "You know why, Uncle Beau."

Yes, he did. But it was fun to push her buttons. "I doubt Summer is going to be in a prom dress, if that's what you're getting at."

"She might be. You don't know."

"I have a pretty good idea."

"If she comes in here in a dress, you owe me ten bucks."

He walked around the desk and stuck out his hand. She shook it heartily.

"Deal," he said. "But where are you going to get the ten bucks?"

"My allowance."

"You must be pretty sure if you're willing to wager your allowance on this."

She shrugged her thin shoulders and tugged on Roo's leash. The big dog turned around and pulled Mary out the door and up to the cash register, bushy tail wagging. He heard Cora groan from up front.

"Mary, you know you're not supposed to have her pull you around on those!"

"But it's *fun*!"

Beau smiled. He had to admit, the banter around here was kind of nice. It filled the silence. He wasn't used to anything filling the silence. He was used to space and quiet hours, his own thoughts echoing through his head.

"Beau," Poppy called, her voice more singsong than usual. "Summer's here!"

He stuck his hands in his pockets and walked out to see Summer standing there talking to his cousins. And damn if she wasn't wearing a sundress with delicate spaghetti straps over her freckled shoulders.

Turning, he caught Mary looking smug from across the room.

"So... I think we'll just get out of your hair," Cora said. "Right, Poppy?"

Poppy smiled at Beau. Then at Summer and back again.

"Right?" Cora repeated.

"Oh! Right. Right. We'll just get out of your hair. Let you and Beau talk business."

He gave them a look as they walked quickly past. They were so full of it. There was absolutely no reason why they needed to leave him and Summer alone, except maybe to fan the flames a little. And Mary wasn't any better. She skated by, wiggling her eyebrows at him.

When his gaze met Summer's, she smiled warmly. He liked that smile. He liked knowing he might've gained her trust a little. What that meant in the long run, he had no idea, but he liked it just the same.

"Hey," she said. "Nice hat."

"Thanks. My sponsor sends boxes of clothes every now and then. I have some T-shirts that would probably fit you. Want one?"

"I'd love one actually. I'll represent you."

He could think of worse things than having his name on Summer Smith's back.

"The coffee table is in my truck," she said. "I'll have the dresser ready next week, but you'll need to pick that up. It's too heavy for me to lift."

"Just let me know when to come get it. We can't keep your stuff stocked, you know. As soon as we get something in, it's gone the next day. And with furnishing this house in Eugene… You'll be busy."

"Busy is good. If it keeps up like this, I might be able to quit my job at the coffee stand. Or at least ease off a bit."

He stepped closer. He could smell her perfume and it made his blood heat. Made him think of things he'd been trying hard not to but was failing miserably at. "How's it going?" he asked. "Have you seen that SUV again?"

"No, thank goodness. Nothing. But I put the cameras up and that makes me feel a little better."

"And how's Tank?"

"He's doing pretty well. He pulled through like a champ. My vet was out this morning and he said if I end up needing to, I can board Tank at his place for a while. So at least I've got a plan if it comes to that."

"Hopefully it won't."

They stood there for a minute as the front door of the antique shop opened with a tinkle of the bell. A group of women walked in, laughing and talking in low tones.

He and Summer looked over at them then back at each other. He could tell she was getting ready to leave, but he didn't want her to. Not yet.

"So…" he said.

"So."

"Your birthday is coming up."

"It is."

"Are you planning on doing anything for it?"

"Well, my parents are coming for a visit, but they have to leave before my actual birthday. My dad has to have carpal tunnel surgery, and that's the only time his doctor could do it or else he'd have to wait until fall. And Angie is going to be out of town, so I'll probably just hang out with my goat."

He smiled. Then remembered what she'd said about this Eric guy and her birthday. Would he be crazy enough to pay her some kind of visit?

She chewed the inside of her cheek. "I know what you're thinking."

"What am I thinking?"

"That Eric might be hanging around. Maybe I'll come into town for a few nights, just in case. I mean, who knows if he'll be back, but I'd feel better if I weren't out there alone on my birthday, since he mentioned it in the letter."

"I think that's smart."

She sighed. "Good. Because I can't stop feeling like I'm blowing this out of proportion. Like maybe Tank was an accident after all."

"Trust your instincts, remember?"

"I remember."

"So," he said, leaning against the front counter. Standing this close, he could see the sheen of her eyeshadow, a greenish taupe of some sort. It brought out her eyes, which were pretty enough without makeup, but when she wore it, she looked like a screen siren from the fifties or sixties. He remembered watching movies with

Ann Margaret in them, his grandpa's favorite star, and thought that her lovely curves and silky copper waves had nothing on Summer's.

"So..."

"Word on the street is that I'm pretty good at fishing," he said. "And I happen to know all the good spots around here."

"Oh?"

"What do you say to letting me take you fishing for your birthday? Maybe not what you had in mind for your thirtieth, but I always wanted to teach you how to fish."

She smiled and clasped her hands in front of her belly. "I remember. I was a bit of a princess back then."

"Maybe just a bit." He winked. "But you said you'd come with me if I baited your hook. You didn't want to touch the worms, which is fair."

A lovely pink crept into her cheeks. She looked so pretty right then that it almost hurt to look at her. What was he getting himself into? He hadn't stopped to think about it. He'd just jumped without looking first and that wasn't like him. Beau didn't do anything without analyzing it first, without thinking about the consequences. His life had always been coldly calculating that way. But when he looked at Summer, all he wanted was to step closer and warm himself against her. To let her breathe some life into him.

She watched him, maybe trying to gauge his sincerity. But before he could walk the invitation back, she nodded. "I'd love that," she said.

He was relieved that she'd said yes but anxious at the same time. He had no idea how he was going to feel about this tonight or tomorrow morning, but it was done now. He was going to take her fishing, and he found that all he wanted to do was find the prettiest, most scenic spot for her. Luckily, there weren't many bad spots around Christmas Bay, so he had that going for him.

"Are you sure this is a good idea, though?" she asked. Her expression fell and he was sure that she'd just come to her senses. At least one of them had.

"Hmm?"

"Your shoulder. Is it up to fishing?"

"My shoulder..." he repeated, hardly able to believe she wasn't shutting him down after all. "Yeah. I'll be careful. The exercises I'm doing mimic some casting movements anyway. I just have to take it easy. But to tell you the truth, I've been dying to get back out there. I miss it."

"I know you do."

The group of women across the shop laughed together at something one of them said. The sun was shining through the window, lighting the entire space in gold. The warmth felt good, but what felt the best to Beau was that he was talking to Summer again. That she'd said yes, despite all the reasons she had not to.

"I'm glad you're coming," he said.

"I'm glad, too."

"And I'll bait your hook."

She smiled. "I wouldn't have it any other way."

Chapter Eight

"Are you sure this is a good idea?" Angie asked.

Summer sat in her truck in front of Earl's Antiques with her phone to her ear, watching tourists walk by. She was still riding the high from Beau asking her out. But the more she thought about it, the more she wondered if this was a date after all. Probably not. Right? He was being nice. It was a birthday outing with an old friend. Still, her heart was pounding, her cheeks were flushed. She could feel the heat in them, the excitement in her belly, which made her uneasy. Getting excited for anything having to do with Beau wasn't a good idea. In fact, it was the worst idea ever, something Angie seemed to agree with.

She took a deep breath, letting it saturate her lungs before letting it out again. She just needed to sit for a minute and clear her head. Angie was always good at talking her down.

"No," she said evenly. "It probably isn't."

"Is it a date?"

"I'm not sure. I don't think so. But then again…"

"How did he ask you?"

"He just brought up my birthday—he knows how

much I love my birthday—and asked about it. It was pretty sweet actually."

"Summer." Her friend sounded stern on the other end of the line. "This is Beau we're talking about here. The jerk. The one who broke up with you for no good reason and shattered your heart."

Summer rubbed her temple. "I know. I shouldn't have said yes."

"I mean I get it. He's gorgeous and successful and all that. But he doesn't do relationships. At least, he didn't when you dated, and he's still single, so what does that tell you?"

Angie was right. Summer knew she was, but she wanted to believe that he'd changed. But had he really? He had major baggage and she'd experienced his issues firsthand. He'd never made her believe that he intended to change, or even wanted to change, so why would he now?

She lay her head back against the rest and looked over at the antique shop. He'd been so complimentary about the coffee table, telling her it was beautiful more than once. He had a way of making her feel special, he always had. And then there was the fact that he'd come out to check on her the other day and had stayed with her when she'd needed him most. If that wasn't some kind of change, she wasn't sure what was.

Still, it was just scratching the surface. She'd needed more from him before, and he'd been unwilling to give it to her. Things were only more complicated now that they were older, more established in their lives and routines. She knew exactly what she wanted and didn't want in a partner, and a man who couldn't meet her halfway wasn't on the list. No matter how successful. No matter how gorgeous.

"Summer?" Angie said. "Are you there?"

"I'm here. Just thinking."

"I'm sorry to rain on your parade. I know how you feel about this guy."

"Felt," Summer said. "Past tense. And it's okay. I just needed a reality check."

"Well, maybe you should go on this date that isn't a date. See what happens. I just don't want to see you get hurt."

"I know and—"

She stopped short when the antique shop door opened and Mary, Beau's adorable niece, came walking out. The girl looked up and down the street and, when she saw Summer sitting in her truck, she broke out in a wide grin and waved.

Summer smiled and stuck her arm out the open window to wave back. Mary began walking toward the truck, her long legs pale in the afternoon sun. Her cutoffs were frayed, and her purple T-shirt was oversized, nearly swallowing her whole.

"Angie," Summer said, "I need to run, but I'll call you tonight, okay?"

"Okay, don't forget. I worry with that creep around."

Summer hoped Eric was back in Eugene and not anywhere near Christmas Bay. But, like Angie, she worried, too.

"I won't. Love you."

"Love you, too."

She hung up and tossed the phone on the passenger

seat just as Mary walked up to the truck and leaned her knobby elbows inside the open window.

"I just wanted to tell you that Uncle Beau doesn't usually dress that slouchy," she said. "He usually looks pretty good. For being old."

"Well. He's not *that* old."

"Yes, but he is slouchy."

Summer laughed.

"He'd kill me if he knew I came out here," Mary continued. "But you're so nice. I just thought I'd tell you that I think he likes you. You know, in case he messes it up by being grumpy. He can be grumpy sometimes."

"I remember that about him," Summer said.

"When you guys were dating?"

Summer nodded.

"My mom said he broke up with you to fish, which is dumb. Just so you know."

"Well…thank you."

"We all think so. My mom, my aunt and me."

Summer smiled. "It sounds like he's outnumbered."

"Yeah, he kind of is. Even Roo is a girl."

"Definitely outnumbered."

Mary stood there for another few seconds and Summer was struck by how tall she was. If she kept growing like this, she could be a model by the time she was a teenager. She took after Cora with her delicate pale skin. She was so cute, so unfiltered, that she'd already wedged a special place in Summer's heart.

"Well," Mary finally said. "I'd better get back."

"Thanks for coming to say hi."

"You're welcome. Are you going to let Uncle Beau take you fishing?"

"I think so. I mean I said yes. But I'm a little nervous."

"About him being grumpy?" Mary patted Summer's arm like a grandmother might. "It's okay. He likes you."

Without another word, she turned and ran back down the sidewalk, her skinny arms pumping. Summer watched her go, thinking about what she'd just said. *He likes you.* She wondered how much of that was the truth and how much of it was eleven-year-old wishful thinking. Mary was a matchmaker at heart. That was obvious. A budding romantic. Otherwise, why would she even have come out to let Summer know that?

Still, the words were like a warm blanket. And even as Summer tried not to think too much about their true meaning, she exhaled softly.

Maybe a little dreamily.

It had been a long day. Summer yawned and stretched then reached for the remote beside the couch and turned off the TV. It hadn't been a very good movie anyway and she could barely keep her eyes open.

She stood up and padded to the bathroom to wash her face and brush her teeth. A storm had blown in late that afternoon, a few hours after her visit to Earl's Antiques, and the wind was busy rattling her old single-paned windows. No rain yet, but that would probably come later. Showing up in the middle of the night to wake her from a dead sleep.

She loved her house, loved living in the countryside, but sometimes it could be a little nerve-wracking. She wondered if she would've felt this way before Eric had shown back up. Maybe. Maybe not. But there was no doubt that the hairs stood up on the back of her neck at the smallest sound outside when, before, she'd been comfortably numb to the wind and rain coming in off the ocean during a storm.

She stepped inside her bathroom and flipped on the light. Then tied her hair back and looked at herself in the mirror. *Pretty enough for all practical purposes...* That's what her grandmother used to say whenever Summer would complain about her freckles or her wild, curly hair, which she'd hated as a kid. Of course, as compliments went, it had been a pretty poor one. Summer had struggled with her self-esteem growing up. She didn't look like all the other little girls with their sleek hair and golden skin. When those girls showed off their tan lines in the summer, she'd have a sunburn. When they curled their hair for dances, she would try to straighten hers, and that was always a disaster.

It was only as she got older that she'd started appreciating her differences. That she'd stopped comparing herself to other women so much and embraced what Mother Nature had given her. Beau had helped with that. He'd always made her feel beautiful and special. And when he'd broken up with her, those old demons had raised their ugly heads again, trying to make her believe she wasn't good enough, or pretty enough, for someone like him. It was silly, of course, but Summer had learned that things didn't always have to make sense in order to affect you deep down.

But as she looked into her green eyes—*Just like the hills of Ireland*, her mother had told her once; she'd been better at compliments than her grandmother had been—she tried to see herself through Beau's eyes. She'd grown up. She felt older and wiser now, thanks to her experiences. The good ones and the bad ones. She wondered what Beau saw when he looked at her, and if he was still attracted to her. Or if that had gone the way of his commitment to their relationship. Long gone, long forgotten.

She ran her hands down her hips and studied herself. They were wider now, her breasts fuller. And she had a tummy where she'd never had one before. The result of her love of late-night snacking and mochas with whipped cream. She could definitely tone up, or maybe start running. Or at least start walking, which wasn't as hard on her knees, which had always been a little wonky. She wondered what Beau thought of her body now and hated that she was wondering. Why did she care? But she knew the answer to that—she cared because of what Mary had said that afternoon.

She sighed and turned on the water, waiting for it to warm up. The wind rattled the windows, howling around the house like it was trying to find a way inside. Shivering, she washed her hands, trying not to think of every horror movie she'd ever seen where the heroine was attacked in the bathroom. Blissfully unaware. Usually with soap in her eyes.

She washed her face quickly, rinsed it then reached for the washcloth on the counter. She patted her face dry, but froze when she heard a sound against her bedroom window.

She stood there, heart in her throat, washcloth pressed to her lips, and stared at herself in the mirror. Her eyes were wide and fearful. The look in them made her stomach turn. She waited, straining to hear past the wind outside, which shook the house with each gust. Maybe she'd just imagined it.

But then, before she could hang the washcloth back on its hook, there was another tapping sound against the glass.

Tap, tap, tap.

She sucked in a breath. There was no imagining that.

She stood there, frozen in place, before finally forcing her gaze away from the mirror and into her darkened bedroom. There was a small strand of twinkle lights over the bed, which provided the only light, enough to cast long shadows over the room. The curtains were sheer but double thickness, so nobody could see in. Yet if someone were standing right outside, they'd be able to see the bathroom light on. And probably the shape of someone standing at the sink.

With her heart pounding, she reached over and batted the light off. Darkness enveloped the room and she blinked a few times, desperate for her eyes to adjust.

Tap, tap.

"Oh my God," she whispered.

Struggling for an even breath, she scanned the bed for her phone. And then remembered leaving it on the charger in the living room. *Damn, damn, damn.* Her stomach sank. She had an appointment to have a landline put in next week. Of course, she'd probably be dead by then.

She shook her head, trying to calm down. She had to get a grip. She needed to check the cameras outside before calling the police. She was scared, and thought she had good reason to be scared, but she was also present enough not to want to call an officer out on a wild-goose chase. Christmas Bay was a small town, and the last thing she needed was word getting around that she was a few donuts short of a dozen.

Forcing a deep breath, she stepped into the bedroom, watching the curtains as the wind continued shrieking outside. If she crossed the room to turn off the twinkle lights, she might be able to see someone's shadow if they were standing outside. The porch light and the light from Tank's shed would definitely be enough to illuminate the shape of a person. But the problem with that, of course, would be crossing the room and getting close to the window, which made her want to throw up.

No, she'd go into the living room, get her phone, and check the cameras. Then, if she saw anything, or anyone, outside, she'd call the police.

Grabbing her Mace—a recent gift from Angie—off the bedside table, she hurried down the hallway, her bare feet padding on the hardwood floor. Rain was beginning to fall outside now; she could hear the drops hitting the roof and slapping against the living room windows.

She narrowly missed tripping over her boots that she'd left beside the coffee table but then promptly stubbed her toe on a stepstool she'd been meaning to take to Goodwill for weeks now.

"Ouch!"

She grabbed her phone off the charger and limped over to the couch to sit. Her toe throbbed and her mouth was so dry it was hard to swallow. All she could think of was downing a glass of water, but there was no way she was going into the kitchen where she knew the sheer lacy curtains were open over the sink.

With trembling hands, she opened the security camera app and held her breath.

From the video on the front porch, she saw sheets of rain illuminated by the bluish light from the porch. The wind rocked the hanging baskets back and forth, the flowers bowing their fragile heads against the onslaught. She saw Tank's shed and darkness beyond. She couldn't see anyone anywhere, but resisted relaxing even a fraction. She still needed to check the back camera, where her bedroom was.

She selected that video and narrowed her eyes at the image. More sheets of rain, more darkness. But at the edge of that…at the very edge…

Summer's throat closed. At the edge of what she could see clearly, there was a shadow. A moving shadow.

She had to call the police now. She just hoped she hadn't waited too long.

Beau lay on the pullout sofa in the living room and stared at the ceiling. The power had gone out a few minutes ago and rain lashed at the windows of the little apartment above the antique shop.

He looked over at the clock on the microwave: 12:24. Cora, Mary and Poppy were sound asleep in their bedrooms, but he'd been tossing and turning on the couch for the last hour. When they'd moved in, it had made sense that his cousins take the bedrooms and Beau take the couch. But on nights like this, he wondered if it would've been better if he'd just gotten himself a small place of his own. He felt claustrophobic and restless.

A gust of wind shook the apartment and he pushed himself up to a sitting position to look out the window. They had a great view of the harbor from there and he could see the white-capped swells rolling in from the ocean. The waves slammed themselves furiously against the rocks of the jetty, sending spray high into the air. The lighthouse across the bay threw its long beam over the water then out to the beach and back again. Every now and then its horn would sound, a warning to mariners that went all the way back to the nineteenth century.

Beau watched the dark turbulent water churn underneath the beam of light and felt his skin prickle. The lighthouse horn sounded low and ominous. Like a different kind of warning.

He thought about Summer and wondered if she had power out at her place. He wondered if she was awake right now and, if she was, if she was nervous. Or worse, afraid. He shifted his weight on the couch, but found that no matter how much he moved around, he couldn't get comfortable. His shoulder ached, his arm burned.

He reached for his phone, and pulled Summer's number up. Staring at it, he listened to the rain pelting the windowpanes. He'd followed his instinct when he'd driven out to check on her that day and something had been wrong. Very wrong. If texting her in the middle of the night was going overboard, then so be it. She'd just have to think he was a mother hen.

He brought up their text thread and started typing.

Hey, couldn't sleep. We don't have power here. Just checking on you. Everything okay?

Setting his phone down, he waited for a reply. And wondered what he'd do if one never came. He should probably just assume she was asleep. But when push came to shove, would he really be able to do that? He knew he wouldn't. He'd just sit there and wonder. And worry. And the thought that he was now not only wondering but worrying about Summer made him shift again, trying to get comfortable.

His phone dinged and he picked it up, squinting at the message.

Power just went out here, too. Thank you for checking, that was nice.

He ground his teeth together. She was sitting out there in the dark, in a storm, with a possible stalker lurking around her place. He knew what he wanted to do. He also knew what he *should* do, which was leave well enough alone. Summer was a big girl and, if she needed his help, she'd ask for it. But at the same time, he didn't think she would. He hadn't exactly been someone she could count on in the past. Why would she think she could count on him now?

Without letting himself think about it any more than he already had, he texted back.

Are you okay out there? Be honest.

He waited, watching his screen. The wind gusted, the rain coming harder now.

I can come over if you need me to.

The text bubble came up. She was responding. But then it went away again and he sat there, gripping his phone. Thinking that he'd like to wrap her in his arms right then and make sure she was safe and okay. And that was a revelation for the ages because he hadn't really admitted this, even to himself, until now. There had been flashes, sure. There had been urges to touch her face or to run his hands down her hips. But this was different. This was a longing that went deeper than just a physical need. And that made his offer to come out to her place in the middle of the night all the more dangerous. Did she feel the same way? It was a presumptuous question. He was sure she probably didn't. She had no reason to. He wasn't anything that she regretted losing. But he regretted plenty.

His phone dinged hollowly and he read the text that came through with a cold feeling inside his chest.

I'm okay, she wrote. But thank you anyway.

Summer watched Chief Martinez make his way down her driveway, his taillights glowing red through the wind and rain. The storm had eased some and the power had flickered back on a few minutes ago, but she still felt chilled to her bones and wrapped her sweater tighter around her midsection.

The tapping she'd heard earlier had been nothing but a fallen twig moving against the window. And the shape she'd seen had most likely been a deer, since the chief had seen a small herd of them crossing the driveway when he'd arrived. Summer felt ridiculous, of course, and had apologized profusely for wasting his time. But he was a nice guy, and an even better police officer, and if he'd been annoyed at having to come all the way out for nothing, he didn't show it. On the contrary, he said she should to call whenever she felt the need. This time everything was fine. But next time, it might not be.

She leaned away from the window and looked at her phone again. The text from Beau had been a surprise. She kept looking at it to make sure she'd read it right. Chief Martinez had been sitting there asking her routine questions when it had come through with a ding, and she'd been distracted enough that he'd had to stop and ask if everything was okay.

Thinking about it now, her face warmed. She couldn't allow herself the luxury of wanting Beau, much less needing him. He was being nice, but that's where it ended. Of course, that's where it would end with him. He wasn't the kind of guy who would want to entangle himself with this. She had to handle it on her own, and any temptation to lean on him like she had the other day had to be dealt with the best way she knew how. Thus, her text back—distant, if not a little chilly.

She watched the cruiser turn out onto the highway and disappear into the rain and darkness. She was safe. At least for the time being. Tank was warm and dry in his shed, and there was nobody wandering around her property. She could go to bed knowing that and feeling secure that Eric wasn't watching her house from the darkness beyond.

Even so, the thought of climbing into her bed and turning off the lights filled her with a sense of dread. There was a rush of anger at Eric for making her feel this way. She wasn't sure she could blame him for wanting Beau here with her, but she did anyway.

She realized with a sinking feeling that wanting Beau was something she was simply going to have to live with for a while. Which was fine, she *could* live with it, but she'd also continue fighting it tooth and nail. She'd made that mistake before and it almost broke her in two. She liked to think she was wiser now. Definitely wiser about Beau Evers.

Still, as she walked down the hallway with her sweater pulled snugly around her, she thought about how sweet it had been for him to text tonight. To check on her. That wasn't the Beau she'd known before, the one who'd left her so abruptly for the other love of his life. This was someone different.

Walking into her bedroom, she slipped her sweater off and draped it across a chair. Then climbed into bed with her stomach still heavy with nerves.

She reached up to flip off the twinkle lights, she usually slept the best in a cool, dark space, but stopped at the thought of her room going completely black.

Instead, she tucked the Mace underneath her pillow and scooted down to burrow underneath the covers. She needed the light tonight.

She wondered what Beau would've done if she'd asked him to come over. Where he would've slept, and if he would've been comfortable staying the night at her place. If his offer to be with her had been genuine or just something he'd felt like he needed to throw out there.

Pulling the blanket to her chin, she closed her eyes and immediately pictured him. Smiling that easy, sexy smile. The one that he wore when he finally let his guard down, which wasn't often. She pictured him reaching for her and in her mind, in her heart, she went to him.

She was asleep before she knew it and was dreaming of him in full, bright color.

Chapter Nine

Beau looked over at Summer, who was standing on the riverbank, a Christmas Bay Tiger Sharks' baseball cap shielding her eyes. She had her head bent in concentration, her red hair cascading over her shoulders, its copper highlights catching the early morning sun in fiery ribbons that hurt his heart.

He smiled, watching her untangle the small minnow plug he'd given her for a lure. No worms this time, which she'd seemed relieved about. But that also meant he hadn't had to stand close and bait her hook, which had been an oversight on his part since he was beginning to look for any and all excuses to stand close to her.

"Okay," she said. "I think I'm ready to cast again. That first time was awful. Can you show me?"

Maybe she'd read his mind. Maybe she was looking for an excuse, too, but it didn't matter. What mattered was that his excuse to get close had just materialized like magic.

He walked over and set his pole down on the riverbank. It smelled damp and earthy, the water rushing past in dark currents. It was chilly, the sun had only just come up and hadn't had a chance to warm things up yet. He wore his favorite sweatshirt with the Cast emblem on the back. It felt good being out here, but it felt even better having a fishing pole in his hands again. He'd been to the river since injuring his shoulder but hadn't fished since then, and standing there was like being able to take a deep, cleansing breath.

"So you want to have your fingers in a comfortable position, so you can trap the line easily. Here..."

With one hand, he held on to her pole and put the other over hers next to the reel. Her fingers were soft and warm, despite it being so cold, and his gut tightened. "Put your index finger here. Like this."

She moved her hand underneath his. He could smell her hair, mingled with the earthiness of the river and the woods behind them. She was close enough that if he turned his head, he'd be able to kiss her.

"Like this?"

"Just like that." He licked his lips, having a hard time getting the thought of kissing her out of his head. "Now once you've got your hand in a good spot on the pole, you can focus on your casting. Since there's a pretty good current, you'll want to cast upstream, so the bait will float down to your target."

"Do we know where the fish are?"

"That's the million-dollar question." He leaned closer and nodded toward a dark spot in the river. "See that spot over there? Where the water is more still?"

She nodded.

"That's a pool, pretty deep by the looks of it. There are probably some guys in there waiting for their breakfast."

She planted her feet apart and took a deep breath.

"Okay," he said. "The fish are facing the current, so like I said, you'll need to cast upstream so the lure will float down to them. Pick a spot and cast toward it. You don't want to let go too early or too late, the point of release affects the height and direction of your cast. You'll find your sweet spot the more you practice."

The corner of her mouth tilted. "You make it sound so easy."

"Well, I've been doing this a while. Ready? You'll want to use both hands."

"Like this?"

Again, he put his hands over hers and slid them gently apart. "You just don't want them to be too wide. This is good."

Her sweater sleeves were pushed up, exposing her wrists. He watched goose bumps pop up on her skin. He wondered if she was feeling the same spark that he was.

Reluctantly, he let her go and bent over to grab his fishing pole. "I'll show you if I can keep my shoulder socket in place."

She frowned. "Oh. Are you sure that's a good idea?"

"My physical therapist gave me the green light to start some light casting if I'm careful."

"Yes, but..."

He winked at her. "Don't worry. If I rip something or pop something, or something explodes, you'll know it. But I'll be fine. Promise."

He gripped the fishing pole, the cork feeling familiar and warm in his hand. Carefully, he raised his arm over his head and, in one fluid motion, cast his line upstream. The spinner arced through the air and landed with a plop on the other side of the river. His shoulder hurt, but it wasn't unbearable. It was more like a tightness that he knew would work itself out with time and exercise. This was good. This was really good, he thought as he exhaled and looked over at Summer, who seemed equally relieved.

"See?" he said. "Nothing exploded."

"You say that, but I was half expecting it to."

He laughed. "If anyone's shoulder could spontaneously combust, it would be mine."

"Showoff."

"Now it's your turn."

"I'm not going to be able to get mine all the way across. Last time it ended up in the weeds over there."

"That's what practice is for. Now show me what you've got."

A light breeze made a few strands of her hair blow across her face. She frowned in concentration as she lifted her pole with both hands, and he didn't think she'd ever looked more lovely. She might just be a natural at this. Only time would tell, which meant one thing—he'd have to take her fishing more often.

She cast and, this time, her spinner ended up in the middle of the river. Not quite across it, but not in the weeds, either.

She beamed. "I did it!"

"Of course you did. There was never any doubt."

Biting her lip, she watched the line move downstream with the current.

"So, you know what a nibble feels like?" he asked, trying not to stare at her plump bottom lip between her teeth.

"Not really."

"It kind of feels like a vibration on your line. A little tickle. If you keep the line between your thumb and index finger, you'll be able to feel it easier. Like this."

Again, he put his hand over hers and positioned the line over her finger. This time, the electricity between them just about hummed. She looked up at him and he was standing so close that he could make out the pattern of her freckles across her nose. Could see her pupils dilating just a little. Could see the tapping of her pulse at the hollow of her throat.

There was a falling sensation in his stomach. His hands itched with the temptation to wrap them in her hair—that coppery mane that he knew would feel like cool silk against his skin.

Clearing his throat, he stepped away and concentrated on his own fishing pole. Saying a quick prayer that he wouldn't do something stupid, like try to kiss her. Being attracted to her was one thing. But acting on it was something else altogether. Nothing had changed since college. He still wanted to be a sport fisherman above anything else. And he was still spooked by commitment.

But even as he thought it, he knew there was more to it than that. Time had given him a different perspective, even though he'd been slow to recognize it at first. Having a woman like Summer, and then losing her, had softened him. He knew now that Summer wasn't like his mother, she wasn't a cheater. And she wasn't like his dad, she didn't leave when things got hard.

Beau was the one who'd left. And, to be honest, that spooked him, too. If he couldn't stay with someone like Summer, how would he ever make anything work? Maybe he was destined to be single for the long haul.

Which wouldn't be so bad, except he wasn't sure he wanted to be a bachelor for the rest of his life. He wasn't sure he liked the idea of being alone for the long haul, which was a far cry from how he used to feel.

He stood there on the damp riverbank, his boots sinking into the soft, dark earth, with Summer standing beside him. Shafts of golden sunlight poured through the canopy of evergreen branches overhead. Tiny gnats buzzed through the air and birds sang a light chorus all around them. It was a nice moment, something he realized he hadn't experienced in a very long time. Maybe since his grandfather had taken him fishing as a kid. Those had been good days, days when he'd enjoyed the beauty and serenity of the river the most. When he'd been happy and comfortable in his skin.

He raised his arm and cast again, and this time there was less pain in his shoulder. He realized that being out there with Summer was bringing that feeling of serenity back, and that he was looking at the river this morning through a different lens—one of being content in the moment. One that made him take a deep breath as he watched his line float down the current toward Summer's.

"Can I ask you a question?" she said after minute.

He nodded but didn't look over at her. He was worried if he did, something might come loose inside him.

"Do you think you would've come back here if your grandpa hadn't passed?"

He narrowed his eyes at the water, sparkling now with the sunlight hitting it. The currents weren't so much dark anymore as emerald green. He could see the river rock at the bottom of the pool where their spinners sat and the shadows of fish waiting there.

He exhaled, the feel of the fishing rod in his hand centering him.

"That's a good question," he said. "I'm not sure."

Out of the corner of his eye, he could see her nod and then adjust the cap on her head.

"How about you?" he asked. "Would you have moved here if you'd had a better experience in Eugene?"

"I'm not sure, either."

She paused. Long enough that he looked over at her. Some color had risen on her face and she was chewing the inside of her cheek. Again, he had trouble keeping his gaze off her lips, which were full and pink in the morning light.

"But I'm glad I did," she finished evenly. And then she looked at him and their gazes locked.

Beau felt his heartbeat hammering in his neck. He watched her hair move in the breeze, catching the sunlight and making his mouth dry. The temptation to touch her, to hold her, was almost too much to resist and he wondered briefly what she would do if he stepped closer. Would she move away? Or would she look up at him with those mossy eyes and part her lips, and let him kiss her like he was dying to?

"Summer..." His voice sounded different. He sounded like someone who might be on the verge of saying something significant.

But before he could go on, the tip of her fishing pole jerked and bent forward.

Her eyes widened. "Oh...oh! I think I might have something..."

He put his hand on the small of her back and looked out over the water. He felt himself grinning like an idiot at her obvious excitement. Putting his other hand on her pole, he felt the unmistakable vibration of a fish on the line.

"Okay," he said. "You definitely have a bite. Just hold on and reel it in."

"I've got something? I've got something!"

He laughed. "Just reel it in nice and slow. It feels big. I think you might have a nice-sized boy."

"Or girl, you never know."

"Or girl."

"I guess now is a good time to tell you that I don't eat fish."

The breeze moved her hair against his face. It made him feel twenty-years-old again.

"That's what catch and release is for," he said.

"Oh good. Because I definitely don't want to kill it."

"No, this fish is gonna live to see another day. Just keep reeling it in."

She brought the fish in like a pro and as it neared the riverbank, it jumped out of the water. The sunlight caught its brightly colored scales, the distinctive ribbon of pink and green.

"You've got a rainbow trout," he said. "And it's a pretty one, too."

"*Ooohhh.* I'm having so much fun. Have I said that yet? How much fun I'm having?"

He smiled. "You haven't, but I'm glad. You're good at this, you know. The whole fishing thing. I think you missed your calling."

"I think you're my good luck charm."

The fish jumped again and this time Beau grabbed his net from the bank, scooping it up as it flopped and struggled.

He leaned down and lifted it out of the net, his fingers pressing gently into its cool, wet body. "Is your phone handy? We can get a quick picture before we let him go."

She pulled it out of her back pocket and scooted next to him as he handed her the fish.

"Here you go. Just hold on to it like this."

He took the phone and put his arm around her. The river sparkled behind them, the sun creating a golden arc in the camera, and he smiled.

"Say cheese."

At the last minute, she looked up at him and grinned, her hat crooked, her eyes twinkling.

And he knew it was a keeper.

Summer sat across from Beau in the little diner booth waiting for their food to arrive. They were starving, so they'd decided to grab a bite before they headed back to town, and she was glad. It was the first time that they'd had a chance to sit down all day, and she realized how tired she was.

Beau watched her from across the table. He'd taken his hat off when they'd walked inside, and there was a flattened ring around his blond hair. But it didn't matter—everything about Beau was sexy. From his bright blue eyes to his strong, stubbled jaw. To the way he was looking at her now—differently but the same. It felt like there'd never been a time when Beau hadn't been a part of her life. Because even when he'd broken up with her, his memory had remained. And she'd gone on to compare every man she'd ever dated to him.

Beau was the love of her life, but that was her great secret. And even though their relationship was long past, she knew he still had the power to break her heart, which was enough to leave her breathless now. Sitting there, sipping her iced tea, trying to act like she wasn't falling for him again.

He leaned forward, putting his elbows on the table. The muscles in his tanned forearms moved underneath his skin. The fine hairs there were bleached blond by the sun. She imagined what they would feel like underneath her fingertips, soft and downy. She pictured the hair on his chest, the same golden color, sliding underneath her hands, and she swallowed hard.

"What are you thinking about?" he asked, his mouth curving slightly. This used to be a favorite question of his when they'd lie in bed together, looking at each other in the dark. She remembered putting her hand on his face once, her heart pounding out a heady rhythm. She'd realized then how much she'd loved him. And that he probably wasn't going to stay. Even though he'd never cheated, never strayed, Beau's heart wasn't hers. She'd known almost from the beginning that it belonged to the river, to the lakes, to the wilderness. He hadn't wanted to be tied down to anyone or anything, and when he'd finally walked out the door, she'd been broken but hardly surprised.

"What am I thinking...?" She looked down at her hands on the table, knowing full well she wasn't going to tell him, but also knowing that he might have an idea anyway. Summer had never been good at hiding how she felt. She usually wore her heart right on her sleeve, a curse of epic proportions.

"I'm just thinking about what I ordered," she finished.

He leaned closer. She caught the faint scent of after-shave and it made her dizzy with longing. When had she lost control of herself so completely? When she'd come into the antique shop and seen him that first morning, she'd been so confident of her disdain for Beau. Or at least her indifference for him. Now, she struggled to maintain eye contact for fear that she'd say something she couldn't take back.

"Liar," he said, his lips tilting.

She looked up, her pulse skipping in her wrists. "What?"

"You're thinking about that fish."

She laughed. "How'd you know?"

"Just a guess. And you have an eyelash." He leaned across the table and brushed his thumb lightly across her cheek. "See?"

She looked at the lash balanced on the tip of his thumb, her skin still tingling from where he'd touched her.

"Make a wish," he said.

She leaned forward and blew softly until the lash disappeared and Beau smiled.

"Don't say what it is or it won't come true," he said. "That's what Mary says, at least. And she's pretty smart for an eleven-year-old."

"She's very smart."

He leaned back in the booth and studied her for a few seconds. Like he was trying to decide what to say next. The muscles in his jaw bunched and relaxed.

"Speaking of Mary," he finally said, "I've been meaning to ask what she said to you the other day."

"The other day…at the shop?"

He nodded and her belly curled. She knew exactly what he was talking about. When Mary had run out to her truck to tell her that Beau liked her. Such a sweet, little-girl thing to do. But the truth was, what she'd said had been hard to shake. Because if it was even partly accurate, then they were playing with fire, she and Beau.

"She…she, uh…" All of a sudden, it felt like the room was smaller. And warmer.

"She…?"

Summer looked down and ran her index finger around the lip of her glass. Their server came to refill their water and to tell them their sandwiches would be right up, but all of a sudden she wasn't hungry. The knot in her stomach was too big. Who knew it would be this hard to open up a can of worms?

He smiled. "Now you've got me interested. What'd she say? Or do I want to know?"

"I'm not sure you do."

"Try me."

"She just came out to tell me…that you like me."

He watched her from across the table. She took a sip of her tea and hoped he couldn't see that her hands were shaking.

After a few seconds, he shook his head and her heart sank. Naturally, he'd want to clear this up. Put a stop to whatever it was. And she should want the same thing. It was the smartest thing after all.

"Summer…" he began.

"No, no. It's okay. You don't have to say anything.

Mary's smart, but she doesn't know everything, right? You just wanted to know what she said, and that was it. No big deal."

Before she could lean back and increase the distance between them, which she was now desperate to do, he reached out and caught her wrist. The feel of his skin on hers sent wave after wave of heat through her.

"She was right," he said, his voice low.

Summer stared at him, unprepared for this. For the boldness of the statement. For the honesty of it.

They sat there, the diner humming around them. And, finally, he slid his hand off her wrist, leaving her cold all over.

"Only," he said, "'like' isn't really the right word."

He frowned then, looking like the brooding Beau she knew so well. That she remembered with a painful squeeze of her heart. She waited, holding her breath for what he might say next.

"I'm not sure what *is* the right word," he said. "I've been thinking about it, though. I've been thinking about you, about us. How things ended between us."

He let his gaze fall to her mouth and it was like he'd physically touched her there. Her lips tingled.

"I'm sorry, Summer," he said. "For walking away from you like I did. I know it's a dollar short and a day late, but I owe you that much."

Beau had a hard time admitting when he was wrong. He always had. The fact that he was doing it now, after all these years, had her reeling.

"Beau…"

"You don't have to say anything. I just wanted you to

know. I don't expect you to forgive me, but I hope you know I mean it. From the bottom of my heart."

"Why?" she said. "Why now?"

Their server set their sandwiches on the table, forcing them to lean away from each other for a second. The food looked delicious—two juicy BLT's on thickly cut white bread with french fries on the side, but Summer still wasn't hungry. She was too invested in the answer to her question. She'd been waiting a long time for this, and now, here it was.

Beau's jaw bunched as the server walked away. He waited a beat, and then took a deep breath. "I think because being away from fishing for a while has changed my perspective. That, and losing my grandpa. Life is so short, and I realized the other day that I never tried to make it right with you. I never apologized for something that I should've owned from the beginning. And for what it's worth, I do remember us talking about moving in together."

"You do?"

He gave her a small smile. And she thought it looked a little sad. "Of course I do. We talked about it that night after the movie, when we were walking home. You were wearing a blue dress and your mother's locket that she gave you for Christmas. The silver one."

Summer felt her heart thump-thumping… If she didn't know better, she'd think she was dreaming. One of those reoccurring dreams she'd have every now and then, where Beau told her he loved her. Asked her to wait for him. And she would've. She would've waited forever.

Her eyes stung and, to her horror, she realized that tears were balancing on her bottom lids. She brushed them away with the backs of her knuckles. "I'm sorry. Just emotional."

"Don't be sorry."

"Well," she said. "Thank you. It's nice to hear. I was kind of crushed when we broke up. I'm not sure if you knew that."

His expression tightened. "I heard through the grapevine."

"I didn't want you to know, so I tried to act like I didn't care anymore. But that was easier said than done. You know how it is with first loves and all that." She smiled, trying to lighten the mood, but it was too late. She'd said more than she'd meant to. Until now, she'd managed not to use the *L* word, but now it was hanging there between them, heavy and meaningful, and too difficult to ignore.

"Yeah," he said. "I know exactly how it is..."

They watched each other.

And the silence was deafening.

Chapter Ten

Beau drove the winding mountain road with Summer beside him, looking out the window. He'd asked her if she had to get back at any particular time, and when she'd said no, he'd said he wanted to show her something. It had been impulsive, surprising him. Because what he was going to show her was his secret fishing hole. The one he'd discovered when he was Mary's age and hadn't even told his grandfather about. And he'd told his grandfather damn near everything.

This was a place he used to come to when his life at home was unraveling. When his parents' divorce was imminent and when Poppy's accident had set all their futures on a different course. It had also been a place he'd come to after he'd broken up with Summer. He'd spent hours sitting on the outcropping of rock that hung over the fishing hole. Breathing in the smell of the soil and water and moss. Thinking of her, trying to be alright with his decision to end it. He'd never told anyone he'd done that and wouldn't have admitted it if they'd asked.

But today it felt like, along with the apology he'd finally given her, he owed her something else, too. Something tangible. Something that she could see and touch and smell. That she could come away with and picture when she thought of him in the future. Because it was becoming more and more important to Beau that when she thought of him, she thought of the good things. Not just the painful things. He didn't want pain to be the legacy of their relationship.

Why did he care so much? He wasn't sure, but he did. When she'd said that he was her first love back at the diner, he'd thought that she hadn't just been his first love. She'd been his only love.

She looked over. "It's beautiful out here."

"It is."

"I'm still trying to guess what you want to show me."

"You can't guess. It's secret."

"How secret?"

"Top secret."

"As in, you could tell me but then you'd have to kill me?"

He laughed. "I wouldn't go that far. But I've never shown anyone else before."

"Seriously?"

He nodded.

"Why me?"

"Just because." He couldn't tell her the real reason—that she was becoming someone he wanted to share things with, that he wanted to open himself up to, and that wasn't like him. None of this was like him.

He took another curve, the Subaru hugging it tightly, and turned the blinker on.

He could see from his peripheral vision that Summer was leaning close to her window, looking up at the giant redwoods towering over them. They were spectacular.

"How old do you think they are?" she asked as he turned the car onto a narrow dirt road.

"Thousands of years. Maybe more."

"Some of them could've been here when Jesus walked the earth."

He thought about that. How humbling it was to be a single, fragile human being in the midst of such breathtaking longevity.

The Subaru bounced and rocked over the dips in the road. He'd seen other cars up here before, of course, because despite thinking of this as his secret spot, it wasn't really secret at all and had been discovered by hikers years ago. The park service maintained the road, and there was even a camping spot not far away, but it was quiet today and he could imagine, like he had so many times before, that he was the only one who knew about it.

The car climbed the twisting mountain road and every now and then there was a view of the ocean through the evergreens. Water sparkled in the distance, the sun reflecting off its surface in flashes and bursts of gold.

And then they were at the end of the road. The top of this particular mountainside. There was a tiny parking lot, which was only a lot in the literal sense. There were five spaces, just big enough for motorcycles and compact cars, and Beau pulled in and turned the engine off. The stillness of the woods immediately enveloped the little car, the air soft and cool coming through the cracked windows.

He opened the door and stepped out, and Summer did, too.

She looked around. "Is this what you wanted to show me? It's *gorgeous*."

"It is, but it's not what I wanted you to see. There's a trail over there. Only about a ten-minute walk. Are you game?"

"Let's do it."

They started off on the trail that, like the road, wound through the trees. The dirt beneath their feet was soft and red and left a powdery dust on their shoes. It smelled like forest and salt water, even though they couldn't see the ocean from where they were.

He watched Summer walking ahead of him, and he could hardly believe he was there with her after all this time. He never would've predicted this, but then again, there were a lot of things in his life that he'd failed to predict. Maybe that was his problem. Maybe he needed to stop trying to see into the future and just enjoy the here and now.

She turned and smiled at him over her shoulder. Her cap low over her eyes, her thick red hair cascading down to the middle of her back. As always, he longed to reach out and touch it. To wrap his hands in it and bring her close for a kiss. He imagined himself trailing his lips along her jawline as she tilted her head to the side. Then down her throat to the warm hollow at its base. He imagined breathing her in, moving his hands down to the softness of her hips and squeezing her gently.

"You're awfully quiet back there," she said, stepping over a small log in the trail.

"Just enjoying the view." He hadn't meant to be a smart-ass, but right as he said it, his gaze had shifted to her backside, where her jeans hugged her curves just right.

After another few minutes, the trail turned to the

right and he watched Summer's posture change as she got her first view of the fishing hole.

She gasped, coming to a stop in front of him. "Oh my goodness. It's..."

"Perfect," he said, unable to take his eyes off her.

"It's just about the most perfect thing I've ever seen. Right out of a movie or something."

It had always reminded him of a movie, too. It was technically a wide spot in a mountain stream, a tributary really, that led to two bigger rivers that led to the ocean. It wasn't always full, the snowpack had a lot to do with that. If they'd had a winter without a lot of snow, and a spring with less rain than usual, the water could be so low that the river rock at the bottom was exposed. But Beau knew that with this winter's snow and rainfall, his favorite spot in Christmas Bay would be full of water and at its most stunning with the meadow surrounding it bursting with purple, orange and yellow wildflowers. And he'd been right. The scene in front of them was simply amazing.

Summer turned to him. "I like your surprises."

"I thought you might."

"You fish here?"

"I do. But I also come up here to think. It's so quiet, it's a good spot for that. Came up when my parents divorced. When my cousin had her accident..."

Summer frowned. "The one with her boyfriend?"

He'd told her about it, but he'd never gone into detail. It was still hard for him to talk about. Poppy had been absolutely broken and only the love, patience and understanding of their grandfather had put her back together again. Beau still had dreams about the accident, he'd seen pictures of how the car had looked afterward, a twisted mass of metal and steel. He still got anxious when someone he loved was driving in bad weather. It had been a life-altering event for him, and that, combined with his parents' split, made him expect that the people in his orbit would leave him eventually. It didn't necessarily mean they would break up with him, or divorce him. They could die. And that revelation had left him cold and distant. Deep down, he knew that's why he'd walked away from Summer. Sportfishing had been a convenient excuse and it had fit the bill at the time. Made perfect sense to the part of his brain that was trying to find sense in it at all.

But at the end of the day, what had really happened was that he'd left her before she'd had a chance to leave him. Period.

He nodded. "And after I broke up with you…"

She turned to face him, her arms crossed over her chest. She didn't say anything and he was glad. He didn't feel like there was anything more *to* say. He'd made a mistake, but it was done now and there was nothing to do at this point but move on.

The birds chirped in the trees above and the gently lapping water sounded sweet and familiar to his ears. Summer looked so pretty, standing there with the dappled sun on her shoulders, that his chest grew tight. If he were a more sensitive man, he might've even said something to that effect. But he had a ways to go in that department, and grit his teeth instead.

Tearing his gaze away from her, he looked out over the water. It was the most beautiful color—a perfect combination of blues and greens and grays. He could see all the way to the bottom where the river rock lay and where fish undoubtedly waited in the dark cracks and crevices for a late lunch. He wished he'd brought their fishing poles, but all he'd been thinking about when they'd gotten out of the car was Summer. Lately, she was the only thing he'd been able to think about.

"Have you ever gone swimming up here?" she asked.

"No way. Too cold."

"But it's summer."

"Still freezing."

She smiled, her eyes bright. She looked much younger than her almost thirty years. She reminded him of a high school girl then, all mischief.

"There's only one way to know for sure," she said. Then took off her baseball cap and shook her hair out.

"Summer..."

She didn't respond. Just peeled her T-shirt off as he stood there staring. She wore a crisp white sports bra underneath, nothing overly sexy, but it might as well have been lacy lingerie for the effect it was having on his blood pressure.

"What are you doing?" he asked, his voice hoarse.

She kicked off her tennis shoes and unbuttoned her jeans to work them down over her hips. Her underwear matched her bra, plain and white, but the cut was as skimpy as a bikini and he felt his mouth go dry.

"I've always wanted to swim in the mountains," she said. "It's a bucket list item. Who knows when I'll get another chance?"

"Well, you live here, so you could come up any time you want."

"But I'm up here now."

"You'll catch pneumonia." He sounded like his grandmother. Here was a gorgeous woman getting practically naked right in front of him and he was basically telling her to put her clothes back on. He bit his tongue to keep himself from saying anything else.

She laughed. "I'm not going to marinate in it, Beau. I'm just going to take a dip. You could join me, you know."

He stared at her. The Summer he'd dated in college had been spontaneous, yes. But this was a whole new level of confidence. It was incredibly sexy, since he was the one who usually made the first move. But was that what this was? Was she making a move? It was impossible to tell, since she wasn't waiting around for him to fumble out a response. Instead, she walked up to the edge of the mountain pool, onto the natural rock overhang.

Turning, she glanced at him over a milky-white shoulder. Her hair cascaded down her back in wild red waves. His heart slammed in his chest, heating his blood. How could he have ever let her go?

"Want to jump in together?" she asked.

"I don't… I'm not…" He tried in vain to remember what boxers he had on. Whether or not they were the ones with the holes that he should've thrown away months ago. And while he was thinking about that, she went ahead and jumped.

He watched the splash with his mouth hanging open. Then walked up to the rock overhang and waited for her to resurface.

When she broke through the water, she gasped. "Holy crap, that's cold!" She laughed, her darkened hair slicked back from her face, the water droplets on her pale skin sparkling like rhinestones in the sunlight.

"I tried to tell you."

"Yes." She looked up at him, treading water. "You did. Good thing I didn't listen."

He stared back.

"Are you coming in or what?" she asked.

"I don't think my underwear is as pretty as yours."

"I won't look."

"Right."

"Chicken."

"Excuse me?"

"If the shoe fits…"

He smiled down at her. "Okay. Alright. Get ready for the cannonball."

She yelped and immediately swam to the side. He unbuckled his belt and dropped his Levi's. "Chicken…" he muttered, giving her a look as he yanked off his baseball cap and tossed it next to his T-shirt.

"One…two…"

She grinned. "Will you just jump already?"

And then he did. Tucking his arm into his side to protect his shoulder, he hit the water next to her, making as much of a splash as possible—a leftover talent from his high school days. It was so cold, it felt like his heart might stop as he kicked his way to the surface. When he broke it, he gasped. "Shit! It's hypothermic!"

She laughed again as he shook his hair, spraying her with water.

He swam over to where she was holding on to a rock.

"You called me a chicken," he said.

"I did. And now I know how to get you to do what I want. Just dare you."

"Basically. But who said I didn't want to?"

"I don't know, you were thinking about it an awfully long time. Nice boxers, by the way."

He cocked his head. "You said you wouldn't look."

"Yeah, well..."

He moved closer and his legs brushed hers. Even with the goose bumps along her skin, she felt impossibly soft underneath the water. It was like brushing up against some kind of sea creature, a mermaid maybe, and he liked that sudden image. It fit. With her hair and her eyes, that's exactly what she reminded him of.

His gaze locked with hers, water dripping into his eyes, blurring them.

She reached up and ran her thumb along his eyebrow. "You're awfully cute, Beau Evers."

"And you're beautiful."

He took in her expression, his eyes dropping to her mouth, suddenly longing to touch her. Taste her. He didn't know how he'd waited this long. He'd been afraid of so many things. But mostly, he'd been afraid of falling for her again.

But he realized, as his lips met hers, that it was too damn late.

He'd already fallen.

Summer leaned back against the slick black river rock, her bottom resting on an outcropping, with the water lapping at her cleavage. But she was hardly aware of any of this. Of the temperature of the water, of the feel of the rock against her body, of her wet hair snaking in thick ropes down her shoulders. The only thing she was aware of at that moment was Beau's mouth on hers, so sexy and tempting. His lips brushed her lips, his tongue nudging them gently open until they were moving in an age-old dance.

She could see the individual points of stubble on his jaw, and his lashes, spiked and dark with water. His shoulders glistening in the sun, his skin golden-tan. He was so gorgeous that he made her breath catch in her throat and she worried for a second that she might not be able to survive this next heartbreak. It felt inevitable. If the pain was anything close to last time, she was in serious trouble.

But she knew, even as she was weighing the risks, that she'd known this would probably happen. She'd wanted it to happen. And now she was going to have to live with the consequences, whatever those might be.

They kissed like that for so long, Summer lost track of time. The only thing she was aware of was Beau. His body brushing against hers, the feel of his hand on her cheek. His scent, making her heady. The way he'd told her she was beautiful, his voice replaying in her head over and over again.

She was tumbling now, down, down, out of control. The fear of getting her heart broken overshadowed only by a longing that was now becoming full-blown lust.

After a few minutes, or maybe more than a few, he finally broke the kiss. He leaned away, but only enough so he could see her face.

"You must be getting cold," he said, his voice low. "You're shivering."

She hadn't realized she was. She wasn't cold, though. She was something else.

He took her hand in his. "Come on. Let's get you out of here."

She let him pull her off the rock and they swam to the side of the fishing hole. Then climbed onto the rocks and out of the water.

Summer sat for a second, hugging her knees in the warm sunshine as the water dripped from her hair down her back.

Beau sat beside her. Her shoulders were probably starting to burn, but for once, she didn't care. She wished she could stay like this forever, here with him, where the outside world didn't matter and neither did their history. She wished they could just start over without any of that in the mix, and see where this day, this afternoon in the sun, would lead them.

But, of course, that wasn't reality. Of course, the world always found its way in. And their history mattered. It was what had led them to this place after all. Sooner or later, they were going to have to deal with it.

Beau turned to her. He was so handsome. "Well, that was fun."

"Really fun."

"I told Cora and Poppy that I'd help with inventory tonight. I should probably get back. But I'd rather stay here with you."

Her heart sank, even though she had to get back, too. She had to feed Tank. And she had a few furniture orders that were waiting. Her life was waiting. But she hated the thought of leaving him, of leaving this moment. There was no telling if it was just a one-time thing, or if it meant more to him than that. She was going to try very hard not to think too much about it, but she knew she would anyway. She'd revisit it over and over again in the days to come.

The question was, Would he?

Chapter Eleven

Summer waited on the second floor of the airport, and looked out the window to the Southwest jet that was taxiing down the runway. Her parents were on that plane and the thought of getting to see them again, of getting to hug them after months of missing them, was enough to make her giddy. Arizona wasn't that far in the scheme of things, but it was far enough, and lately when they'd fly out to visit, they looked older to her. It was a sobering reminder that living in another state meant that she was going to have to get used to longer periods between visits.

Her stomach tightened. She was excited but she was also nervous, and that had everything to do with Beau. More specifically, with the fact that her mom and dad were going to be asking pointed questions about her life, and love life, and she didn't want to lie to them. Or worry them. And they'd most certainly be worried, because they couldn't stand Beau Evers.

It would've been natural for them to have taken a disliking to him after the breakup. But they hadn't even liked Beau when they'd been dating, something that had annoyed Summer to no end at the time. *I love him!* she remembered yelling one three day weekend—the one right before he'd broken the news that he'd be quitting school to fish professionally. She remembered her mom looking at her sadly from across the room during that fight. *He's going to leave*, she'd said. *And then where will you be?*

Summer had resented the implication that he didn't care about her as much as she did him—that's exactly how she'd taken their not-so-subtle warnings at the time. But then her parents' prediction had come true and she'd cried for a week straight. A few of those days she hadn't even been able to muster the energy to get out of bed and her mother had had to come over and practically force her to get out of her pajamas. It had scared her. And quite frankly, it had scared Summer, too.

Her parents had known from the beginning that Beau wasn't going to stick around. They'd tried to get her to see that, too, but she'd been blind to the realities of their relationship. Of his personality, which had always been a little unpredictable, a little distant. But whenever anyone would suggest that he should be prioritizing her more, she'd find ways to rationalize his behavior. His chilliness at times. She understood now that that chilliness had been his way of trying to start the leaving process. He hadn't known how to end it. He hadn't known how to walk away.

She bit the inside of her cheek, and turned to make her way down the escalator to the baggage claim for the Phoenix arrivals. Of course, all these things were ancient history, but as far as her folks were concerned, they might as well have happened last week. Her parents wouldn't understand why she'd be interested in working with Beau, let alone going on a date with him. And at the thought of that kiss the other day, she shivered, knowing she didn't have to tell them the exact details, but also knowing they'd be able to tell something was going on whether she offered any breadcrumbs or not. They'd always been intuitive with their daughters that way, and she'd never been able to get away with anything in high school as a result.

Coming to a stop, she watched as the first of the passengers made their way toward the baggage carousel. Some were greeted by friends and family holding signs or craning their necks for a better view. Others ran, backpacks bouncing, into the arms of their squealing loved ones, making Summer smile. With everything going on, she'd almost let herself forget about Eric. But as she stood there watching the people around her who seemed so happy, she felt a cold shadow cross over her heart. Her parents deserved to know what was happening there, too, but again, she didn't want to worry them. Her mother liked to remind her that even though her baby was getting ready to turn thirty, she was always going to be just that—their baby. The worrying never ended, no matter how old she got.

She knew if she were a parent, she'd want to know.

Finally, she saw the first glimpse of her mom and dad walking toward her, pulling their carry-ons behind them. They looked tanned and healthy from their cruise and they were scanning the waiting area for her expectantly.

Her heart squeezed like it always did when she saw her family after so long apart. She'd tell them about Eric. She just had to find the right time.

* * *

Summer's mother leaned back in the deck chair, the one facing the lush green farmland surrounding the house, and gave her youngest daughter a look.

"I know what you're thinking," Summer said.

"What am I thinking?"

Summer took a sip of her lemonade, the ice tinkling in the glass. She licked the tartness from her lips before setting it down again. "You don't like Beau."

"Well, no. Why would we?"

She had a point there.

"I know," Summer said, resigned.

"We just don't want you to get hurt, sweetheart. And last time…"

"I know, Mom."

"Do you? Because it seems like you're doing an awfully good job of forgetting. And that's all I'm going to say."

Summer knew better than that. Her mom would have plenty to say before this trip was over. Most of it warranted, but still.

"I just don't want you upset by this," she said. "Everything will be fine."

She wasn't sure she believed that, but she wanted to put her mom's mind at ease. She'd done the right thing telling her parents about Beau, because her sister, who she talked to on the phone nearly every day, would probably let it slip eventually. Then her mom would be hurt, and for good reason. But now that she'd told her, she hoped they could move on from the subject. At least for a while.

Her mother wore an expression that said she wasn't done talking about it yet.

"As concerned as we are about you getting involved with Beau again—"

"We aren't exactly involved."

"You're working together, right? That's involved in my book."

Summer frowned. She couldn't argue with that.

"As concerned as we are about that," her mom went on, "we're more worried about this Eric person. This sounds dangerous, Summer. Are you sure the police have it handled?"

"I just got an update this weekend. I guess they questioned him and he's denied coming here at all. So, it's his word against mine. Hopefully, the contact will deter him from anything else."

Her mom didn't look convinced. Which was fine, because Summer wasn't convinced, either. But what could she do? She hated that at this point, Eric was becoming something that she just had to accept, at least for the time being.

"Your father and I have been talking about it and we think you should come back to Arizona with us for a while. Until this blows over…"

"Mom, I can't do that. I have a business here."

"You could restore furniture in Arizona."

"I have a house here. I have bills, a goat to take care of. I can't just leave."

"You could rent the house out. Or make it a vacation rental for a while, those always do well, especially on the coast. And you could find someone to take care of Tank. It would just be temporary, honey. But you're all alone here. What if something happens and we're so far away?"

Summer frowned. She'd thought the same thing about a hundred times, but didn't want to admit it out loud.

"I know you're worried," she said. "But I'll be careful. And Beau offered to let me stay with him and his cousins in town if I need to."

Her mother pursed her lips. "Right. If he sticks around long enough."

"Mom."

"Well, I'm just saying. Since when is he someone you can count on?"

The question was sharp and her mother immediately saw how much it cut.

"I'm sorry, Summer," she said. "I just don't know how to be supportive of this and protective of you at the same time."

Summer took another sip of her lemonade. Her tongue suddenly felt like cotton. "I know it's hard for you to understand," she said. "I'd probably feel the same way if I were you. And I'm not involved with him like that, so you don't have to worry about that part."

Even as she said it, though, she wondered what she and Beau were doing. They weren't dating, but they were practically skinny dipping together? Making out like teenagers? What did that mean exactly? She was playing with fire and she knew it. Her mother knew it, too, but this time she didn't say anything. She just sat back and looked out over the land, rubbing her hands down her thighs.

"Let's talk about something else," her mom said. "I don't want to argue."

"We're not arguing."

"Not technically, I guess. I just want to enjoy the day.

The fact that we get to spend time with you before your birthday."

Summer smiled.

"Which reminds me, what do you want for your birthday, anyway?"

"You and Dad coming to visit is plenty."

"There's nothing you've been wanting? Nothing special?"

Summer felt her cheeks grow warm. What she'd been wanting was Beau. But she couldn't exactly ask for him all tied up with a ribbon, so she shook her head.

"Well," her mom continued, "we're going to take you out for a nice dinner. And if you'd like Beau to come, he's more than welcome to join us."

Summer stared at her.

"What?"

"You just got done warning me off him."

"I know," her mom said evenly. "But you said you two aren't involved like that. Which I don't believe for a minute, by the way. You're definitely in business together though, so we can just call it a working dinner."

Summer wasn't sure how to feel about this. Deep down, she knew her mom wanted to get a good look at Beau again. Probably to try and gauge his true intentions.

Her mother reached out and patted Summer's hand. "You think about it. And if you decide you want to invite him, great. Dad and I will be thrilled."

Summer gave her a look. Her dad was even more skeptical of Beau than her mom was.

"He will be," her mother insisted. "Cross my heart."

Beau walked down the sidewalk with Mary beside him. When she was little, she would hold his hand on outings like this. At least on the few occasions he'd seen her when she was little—his fishing schedule hadn't left him very much time for family, or friends, or anything else. But now, as a tween who would soon be a full-blown teen, she was too old for such things, though she still wasn't embarrassed to be seen with him, which he was counting as a win.

They were headed to Coastal Sweets, her favorite place on the planet, because the lady who owned it, Frances O'Hara, always gave her free gummy worms when she walked through the door. Therefore, Frances was also her favorite person on the planet. The older woman apparently had Alzheimer's, something that was becoming more and more obvious to Beau. She'd forget their names, even though they came in all the time, and conversations they'd had the day before. But she was still managing to work in the shop, thanks to her three foster daughters who took turns working there, too. It was a sweet place, and she was a nice lady, and the candy was delicious. Beau's waistline could attest to this. In fact, he'd sworn off Coastal Sweets for the time being, but Mary had twisted his arm. Or twisted his leg, as she'd called it. She was always messing up sayings. His favorite was "hammy downs" when she meant "hand-me-downs." She hadn't been amused when he, Cora and Poppy had pointed it out one night, hardly able to control their laughter.

She walked next to him now and he thought she'd gotten taller over the last few months. She was definitely going through a growth spurt. Her arms and legs were ganglier than ever, but he knew this awkward phase would pass and she'd grow into them. That she'd look just like her mom in a few years.

She smiled up at him. "Thanks for coming with me. I know you're on a diet from candy or something."

"You didn't have to twist my leg."

"Uncle *Beau.*"

"I know, I know. I'm sorry."

"Sooo, I heard you on the phone this morning…"

He'd lost track of the times she'd listened in on his conversations. Mostly, he was just talking to furniture contacts, so he didn't care. But this morning Summer had called so, of course, Mary had honed in on that.

"What if I wanted that conversation to be private?" he asked as she strategically stepped over every crack in the sidewalk.

"Then you should've closed the door," she said.

Well. She had him there.

"Why did she call?" Mary asked. "It sounded like she was, like, asking you out."

"She was asking me to dinner. Her parents are here for her birthday."

"Are you going?"

"I'm not sure."

"Why not?" she asked.

"Because her parents don't like me."

"Then why would they want to eat with you?"

"Excellent question."

"Don't step on that one!" Mary cried, grabbing his arm. "It's bad luck."

"Don't *do* that. You're going to give me a heart attack."

"You almost stepped on that *huge* crack. Good thing I'm here, or else."

They continued walking, the coastal breeze balmy. It was a gorgeous afternoon and Beau had to admit, gummy worms sounded pretty good right about now. Since when had he turned into the kind of guy who looked forward to gummy worms?

"I think you should go," Mary said.

"Yeah?"

"Yeah. I mean you took her fishing and stuff. It'd be kind of weird not to go to dinner for her birthday. Even if her parents think you're a dork."

"I never said they thought I was a dork."

"Whatever, Uncle Beau. You kind of are. I mean I love you and everything, and you can't help it, but you are."

"Thank you?"

She ignored that. "You should go, and try and be cool, and then her parents might like you."

"I don't know."

"Why?"

"Because fishing is one thing. Dinner with her parents is something else."

"Oh. I get it."

He looked down at her. She wore a knowing expression that reminded him of his grandfather. He used to look just like that when he'd worked something out and was proud of himself for it. Especially where Beau was concerned, because Beau could be a mystery as well as a pain in the ass a good portion of the time.

"You get what, Miss Smarty Pants?"

"You don't want her to think you like her. Which is dumb, because you *do* like her."

There was no use denying that anymore. Ever since

kissing her the other day, he couldn't even deny it to himself, and that was a problem. Because he knew this wasn't how he was going to get back to fishing. This was how he was going to get derailed.

He was starting to feel that same old tug on either side of his heart, the exact one he'd experienced at twenty years old. He felt like Summer was on one side and sportfishing was on the other, and he didn't know how to go both ways. He didn't think he *could* go both ways, and that was the honest truth. He didn't want a leftover relationship—and that's what anything with Summer would be if he was fishing six months out of the year. She'd get what was left of him. And he also didn't want to have a half-assed career. Either he was all-in, completely devoted to fishing—or it would show and he'd never be sponsored again, which would be the end of it anyway. For good this time.

"It's complicated," he finished.

"Not really. Either you do or you don't. Easy peasy lemon squeezy."

Easy peasy. He really needed to close the door the next time he got a phone call from Summer. Or from anyone else, for that matter.

"Uncle Beau?"

"Yes, honey."

"I'm sorry I called you a dork."

"It's okay. I forgive you."

She looked down at her sneakers and, for the time being, it seemed like she'd forgotten about not stepping on the cracks. Her brow was creased and her bottom lip stuck out just a little. She was in deep thought, a shadow crossing her face that was usually so sunny.

"If I haven't told you lately," she said. "I'm glad you're here with us. I mean I know you're not gonna stay and everything, since you want to fish again, but I'm glad you're here right now. You make me think of my dad sometimes."

That got him right in the heart. Like an arrow hitting a bull's-eye.

Gnashing his teeth, he thought of everything he should say right then—how sorry he was about her dad. How he loved her very much, and how proud he was of her. How happy he was to be her uncle.

But all of these things never got a chance to be said because, just when he was about to put his arm around her, she ran ahead. Without him even realizing it, they'd arrived at the candy shop.

"Come on, Uncle Beau!" she yelled from down the sidewalk. "I know you're old, but they're gonna be gone before we get there!"

He knew better than that. Frances kept the gummy worms well stocked. But he broke into his best old-person jog anyway, delighting his niece to no end.

"Coming," he said. "You don't want me to break a hip, do you?"

Chapter Twelve

Summer sat across from her parents at the little Mexican restaurant that she'd always wanted to try but had never had a chance to until now. Beau sat beside her, taking a long sip of his beer. She suspected he was glad he had something to do for a few seconds other than try to make small talk with her mom and dad who, despite promising that they'd wanted to have dinner with Beau, were being fairly stiff.

This hadn't been the best idea in the world. In fact, Summer felt the beginnings of a headache throbbing at her temples and wished they had the check already so she could go home and lie down.

But to be fair, the tension at the table wasn't the only reason why she felt so unsettled. Actually, it wasn't even close. The main reason was because she'd found another note that morning and her heartbeat hadn't returned to a normal rhythm all day.

She took a sip of her wine and shifted in the booth, trying to get comfortable.

Her mother frowned. "Are you okay, honey?"

"Just hungry." She smiled, but she knew her mom probably wasn't buying it.

Beau put a hand on her knee underneath the table and squeezed lightly. Probably thinking she felt the tension between him and her parents and trying to reassure her the best way he could. He'd been hesitant about coming tonight, she'd known that. In hindsight, she should have put the kibosh on the whole thing.

She put her hand on top of his and held his fingers briefly before letting go again. She needed to figure out what she was going to do about the note, other than taking it to Chief Martinez, of course. She didn't feel safe at her house, and hadn't for a few weeks now, and that was starting to wear her down. In her bones, she felt like this whole thing with Eric was going to come to a head and she really didn't want to be alone when it did. Maybe she *should* think about going to Arizona for a while. But there was no telling how long that would be. She had a life in Christmas Bay; she had a business here. And Beau was here, too. But how long would it be until he left again?

She smiled over at him and he smiled back, watching her closely. She hadn't mentioned the note yet, but she'd tell him after dinner. It was one of the most frustrating experiences of her life because, outside of giving Eric a warning, there was still nothing the police could do.

She'd found the note beyond the range of the cameras she'd put up—it had been on the fence post leading up to the house. It hadn't been threatening. It had simply said "Happy Birthday!" With a little smiley face below it. That smiley face had terrified her. She'd immediately gone to check on Tank, who'd been blissfully unaware that anything was wrong. He'd only been interested in his breakfast, which was one good thing at least.

Shifting in the booth again, she took another sip of wine. At this rate, she'd be drunk by the time dinner came.

"So," her dad said, clearing his throat. "Beau. Tell us what you've been doing since moving to Christmas Bay. Summer says you're working at your family's antique shop. That's quite a change from traveling the country as a sport fisherman. How are you adjusting to being in one place for longer than a few weeks at a time?"

Summer detected a tone there and shot her dad a look. Again, she wondered why in the world she'd agreed to this. To be fair, her parents had probably had the best intentions, but when they'd finally sat down face to face with the man who, in their eyes, had wronged their daughter, they just couldn't help themselves. Thus, the tone. And the questions that were just passive aggressive enough to be antagonistic.

Beau set his beer down with a nod. "It's been an adjustment for sure. But I'm actually enjoying being back. It's hard not to be able to fish, but I'm learning a lot about the business, and this is what my grandpa was hoping we would do, so that part is nice."

"We're sorry to hear about your grandfather," Summer's mom said. "That's hard."

"It was. It is. But we're getting through it. Thank you."

"Do you think you'll be here for a while?" Summer's dad asked. "In Christmas Bay?"

It was the question Summer knew her parents were dying to get the answer to. They knew she was involved with him, at least somewhat, and they wanted reassurance that he wasn't going to do the exact same thing he'd done before.

Despite not wanting to care, and feeling the need to give her dad another look, Summer couldn't help but wait for Beau's answer, too.

He paused for a few seconds. And then a resolved expression settled over his face.

"It's my intention to get back to sportfishing as soon as possible. I'll need to help my cousins with the shop for a while, and wait for my shoulder to heal, but soon."

Her dad frowned. And Summer's stomach sank, although she didn't know why. She'd known this had been his plan all along.

"So do you have any idea when that will be?" her dad asked.

"I'm not sure. My physical therapist says things are moving in the right direction, so that's good."

"You'll be traveling then," Summer's mom said. "Will you be coming back to Christmas Bay often?"

Summer watched him. This was the part where, in a perfect world—one where they'd talked this through and had decided to try to make something work—he would acknowledge some kind of relationship between them. Some kind of commitment to her. But she knew this was all just wishful thinking on her part because they hadn't talked anything through. Still, her heart wanted what it wanted. No matter how unrealistic that might be.

Beau took a deep breath. And Summer realized she was holding hers.

But before he could say anything, the waiter appeared out of nowhere with their food. "Who had the carne asada?" he asked with a smile.

* * *

"Your parents hate me."

Beau walked beside Summer down the sidewalk, his hands buried in his pockets. He'd asked if she'd like to get an ice cream before he took her home since it was such a nice evening. Warm with barely any wind. They were headed to Scoop on Sixth, which stayed open later on Saturday nights, its old-fashioned parlor doors propped open for the salty breeze.

She looked over and smiled. "They don't hate you."

"Okay. They *really* don't like me."

"I'm sorry about all the questions," she said. "They're way too protective."

"Well, I get it. You're their kid and they're worried about you. I would be, too, if my daughter was interested in someone like me."

Summer tucked her hair behind one ear. It was loose tonight, cascading past her shoulders in silky sunset waves. She looked down at her feet as they walked. She was wearing what Mary referred to as ballet flats. His niece had multiple pairs that she left strewn all up and down the stairs, which he was definitely going to trip over and break his neck on someday.

She glanced over again, but this time he kept looking straight ahead. What he'd said was true. He wouldn't want his daughter involved with someone like him. Selfish, unable to commit. He wouldn't go so far as to say he couldn't love, because he did. Deeply. And maybe that was his problem. Maybe he was afraid of that depth and what it meant for his heart.

"Don't say that," she said. "You're a good guy, Beau."

He fisted his hands in his pockets. "Am I?"

A family walked by on the sidewalk, a toddler girl hanging on to her mother's hand. She gazed up at Beau and Summer with impossibly blue eyes.

"Hi," she said as they passed. She clutched a melting ice cream cone in her free hand. Chocolate was smeared all over her mouth and Beau's heart lurched, despite himself.

"Hi, there," he said.

After a second, Summer nudged him in the ribs. "You're a softy, Beau Evers. No matter what you want people to think."

"Hardly. I just like kids."

"No, you have a big heart. I know that about you."

"You should actually be calling me a jerk."

Turning to her, he slowed a little.

She slowed, too, and looked over at him curiously. "What?"

"Why *haven't* you called me a jerk? For the way I left when we were getting serious."

She crossed her arms over her chest. "Well, I called you insufferable, remember?"

"Yeah, not the same."

"You act like I'm some kind of saint," she said with a small smile. "I was mad at you for a long time, Beau. I've called you worse than a jerk, if you want the truth."

"Yeah, I figured. But I mean now. Why aren't you angrier now?"

"Do you want me to be angry now?"

"I just want to understand."

She fell into step beside him again. He guessed he wanted an answer because he wasn't sure he deserved this. Any of it. Her forgiveness, or a second chance, if that's what they were going to call it. It all felt fragile, like it could fall apart at any minute. And why wouldn't it? He still wanted to fish. He still wanted to leave. Didn't he?

"You've always known exactly what you wanted," Summer said. "Even if that wasn't me, I got to a point where I respected it. You're a passionate person, and that's something I loved about you. And, truthfully, I still do."

They continued walking, the headlights of the occasional car passing them on Main Street, cutting through the dusky evening. The old-fashioned streetlamps had flickered on a few minutes ago, making their shadows stretch long and thin off to the side.

Beau jammed his teeth together, thinking about what she'd just said. She loved his passion. Did that mean she'd understand when he left again? How many times could she be expected to forgive this tendency of his to run away? *He'd* kissed *her*. He'd opened that door, knowing full well the smartest thing was to leave it closed. Now what?

"I guess what I'm saying," she said, "is that I'm not holding any grudges, if that's what you're worried about."

Her arm brushed against his. It felt right walking alongside Summer. Heading to get an ice cream on a warm night. Even talking about their past felt, if not necessarily good, at least comfortable. All things that he was still getting used to. All things that he wasn't looking forward to letting go of again because, in the end, no matter how good it felt, he was absolutely the type to let it go.

Summer looked over at him. “Let’s not worry about the future, okay? We can just take it as it comes.”

The future. It was the elephant lumbering beside them. And he’d been waiting for her to bring it up. But this… This was like she was letting him off the hook. And he wasn’t sure how to feel about that.

Without responding, because he was absolutely sure he’d screw it up anyway, he put an arm around her shoulders and pulled her into his side. She fit perfectly next to him, like a missing puzzle piece. She was warm and soft, and smelled so good that it hurt.

“All I’m asking,” she said, “is to be honest with me when the time comes, okay? Don’t let me fall…” She didn’t finish. Just let her words trail off on the breeze.

He could imagine what she had been about to say.

Because he felt the same way.

Summer sat on the swing in Christmas Bay Elementary School’s playground, licking her ice cream cone. Mint chocolate chip, her favorite.

Beau stood behind her, pushing her gently, her feet scuffing the sawdust underneath her. She felt like a teenager again. She couldn’t remember the last time she’d done something like this. But more importantly, she couldn’t remember when she’d felt like this—so in love that her heart was in danger of swelling up to twice its size if she wasn’t careful. She really was trying to be just that. Careful and pragmatic when it came to Beau. But she also knew it was basically a losing battle. It had been a losing battle ever since he’d kissed her in that sparkling fishing hole.

She licked the creamy sweetness off her lips and

slowed herself down. The sun was about to set and she felt like she should get home. Her parents were fine on their own, of course, but they could barely work the TV and she felt guilty for being gone for an entire evening of their visit. She felt like she barely got to see them as it was.

Stopping the swing, she scooted off and stood. She still hadn't mentioned the note that was tucked inside her pocket, the evening had felt too nice to spoil it. But she felt like she needed to tell Beau before she went home, for the same reason she'd told her parents about the first note—he'd probably be upset if she didn't.

"I have to tell you something," she said, "but I don't want you to worry."

He frowned. "What is it?"

"I got another note."

Color crept into his face. "Damn it. What do we do now?"

"The police will contact him again, I'm sure. And we keep documenting things until, hopefully, he'll get tired of it and move on."

"And if he doesn't?"

That was the question she was afraid to ask herself. If he didn't move on, would it be like this forever? Was she going to have to live with an undercurrent of unease, if not downright fear, from Eric's constant presence in her life?

"It'll be okay," she said, trying to convince herself as well as Beau.

"How long are your parents here for?"

"Until Tuesday, then they're flying out to see my sister before heading back to Arizona. They want me to come out there for a while, but that doesn't make a lot of sense. Besides, I can't let him chase me away."

"No," he said, his eyes dark in the dusky light. "But you shouldn't be alone right now. Maybe it's time to come stay with us at the shop for a while. Even if it's just for a few days."

"Oh… I don't know."

"Your birthday is this week, and you said yourself you think that's why he's back. Just come stay until after that, and then we can see what happens."

She bit the inside of her cheek. Spending a few nights with Beau didn't sound like the worst thing in the world. But she also didn't want to inconvenience his cousins. The apartment above the shop was small and one more person would probably feel like a lot.

"Is there room?" she asked. "You're sleeping on a pullout couch…"

"If you want your own bedroom, Poppy could bunk with Mary and Cora for a few nights. And this isn't just my idea, they've been worried about you, too. You're more than welcome, Summer. They all care about you."

It was tempting. If she only stayed a few nights, hopefully it wouldn't be too much of an imposition. And who knew? It might just break the cycle with Eric. Maybe he'd see that she had people in her life that she was close to and could lean on, which might be a deterrent. Maybe then she wouldn't be so vulnerable, so much of a target in his eyes. Then again, she wasn't going to pretend to know what in the world went on in his head.

She took a deep breath and wrapped her arms around herself. "Are you sure?"

"Absolutely."

"Okay… Just for a few nights. Thanks, Beau."

He smiled and stepped forward to kiss her on the temple. Something someone who cared about her would do. Something a boyfriend would do.

Her stomach tightened as he kept his lips against her skin for another few beats and then stepped away.

"It'll be nice to have you close," he said.

She was afraid to read too much into that. But her heart squeezed anyway.

Summer watched as Dr. Poet's truck made its way down her driveway, pulling the small trailer behind it, the red taillights blazing through the dusk. She heard Tank bleating from inside and felt fresh tears sting the backs of her eyes. This was the right thing to do. She was sure of it. If she wasn't going to be at her place for a few days, Tank couldn't be there alone.

So she'd called Dr. Poet a couple of days ago and he'd been wonderful, as usual. He'd promised that her goat would be safe and happy on the other side of town with him. And she knew that was true. But it still felt like she was abandoning her pet and that made her mad. The tears threatening now were more anger than anything else, which felt better than the fear. Her parents had left that morning, with her dad offering again to cancel his surgery so they could stay through her birthday, but she wouldn't even consider it.

"No way," she'd said. "I'll be fine, don't worry."

He and her mother had fretted anyway but, in the end, had gotten on the plane with a hug and a kiss and a promise to call her as soon as they got to her sister's place. As much as she was going to miss them, she was glad to be heading to Beau's that evening and staying for the rest of the week. Her mom and dad seemed to have softened toward Beau a little. They appreciated that he'd be there to watch over her, even if it was only temporarily, so that was the silver lining to all of this.

Summer stood there watching Dr. Poet's truck turn onto the highway and saw him reach out the window to wave. She waved back, standing on her tiptoes, until the truck was out of sight and she could no longer hear Tank's cries from the trailer.

Slowly, she turned to walk back toward the house. Warm yellow light spilled from her living room windows and onto the front porch where her wind chimes tinkled softly. Overhead, a flock of sparrows passed in a flutter of wings, their bodies dark and small against the cotton-candy sky. Tank wasn't exactly a guard dog, but without him there, she felt ridiculously alone. Chills marched up the back of her neck as she climbed the old wooden steps to her front door.

Before she reached for the handle, she turned to look behind her. She had the unsettling feeling she was being watched, but that was nothing new these days. Still, the chills made their way into her scalp and her hair prickled with them. She scanned the property, narrowing her eyes at the shapes and shadows in the growing darkness. Just her truck, Tank's shed, her workshop… But the feeling remained and she turned to yank the door open and step inside, hurrying to lock it behind her.

Beau had called earlier, asking when she'd be over. She'd told him she just needed to pack a bag and lock up her shop. He'd offered to pick her up, but she hadn't wanted him to come all the way out and, besides, she needed her truck. Now, though, she wished she'd just accepted his offer. Her house felt cavernous all of a sudden and her heart hammered as she walked quickly into the bathroom to grab her makeup bag and hair dryer.

Stuffing her things in a bag, she forced a deep breath. She hated this. She hated being nervous and afraid, and chased away from her own house. But at the same time, she knew this was her reality for the time being and she was grateful she had someplace safe to go, with people there who cared about her.

At the thought of Beau, she rubbed her lips together as she walked over to the closet to get her clothes. She'd been trying hard to keep this whole thing in perspective, but their kiss had thrown her for a loop. He wasn't planning on staying in Christmas Bay for the long haul, he'd said as much to her parents over dinner. Even though she'd expected it, she hadn't been able to protect herself as much as she'd tried to. She was in love again. Really, she'd never fallen out of love with Beau. And now she needed to figure out what to do about that. She couldn't go through another heartbreak like the last one; it was as simple as that.

The air-conditioning clicked on and her old house creaked as the air shifted inside the room. Summer closed the closet door, catching her reflection in the mirror. Her eyes looked wide and dark, and again she couldn't help but think of a horror movie heroine. There was nobody else in the mirror, but her heartbeat kicked up a notch anyway. She really couldn't get out of there fast enough, and she still needed to go and lock up the shop, something she wasn't looking forward to. She'd take her Mace, but she still felt like a sitting duck as daylight gave way to darkness outside.

Grabbing her purse and putting it over her shoulder with her bag, she headed for the door, checking to make sure she hadn't left the coffeepot on as she went. She switched the living room lights off, stepped out onto the porch and closed the door behind her. Then made doubly sure it was locked.

The wind chimes tinkled a few feet away, but other than that, the night was eerily still. Quiet. There wasn't even the sound of the occasional car going by on the highway to punctuate the silence.

Summer looked around, narrowing her eyes at the inky darkness and trying to see beyond the shadows. Then she hitched her bag up on her shoulder and hurried down the porch steps, hoping she wouldn't fall on her face as she went. That would be all she needed.

She jogged toward the shop. The light from inside blazed through the door that was open a crack. Eyeing it, Summer slowed to a walk, her stomach clenched. She was sure she'd closed it earlier. Well…she was pretty sure.

Swallowing hard, she reached for her Mace. In five minutes, she'd be safely in her truck and headed down the road. But right then, she felt sick to her stomach. She tried to remember her exact routine that afternoon. She'd been working in the shop and she'd come out to get the mail. She always closed the door when she got the mail, because she used that time for a break—usually running inside to use the bathroom and get something to eat. So she'd closed it then. But later, when she'd left her work to meet Dr. Poet… What about then?

She stood in the falsely comforting light that was spilling out onto the gravel driveway, her heart pounding. She just needed to peek inside, make sure nobody was in there, turn off the light and lock the door. Something that would literally take about thirty seconds. Even so, the thought of seeing someone standing there—someone who might turn out to be Eric—made her want to wet her pants.

Gripping her Mace, she forced another swallow. This was ridiculous. This was *her* house. This was *her* shop. She was going to open the damn door and make sure her work was safe inside, and if someone *was* in there… well, they were just going to get a face full of pepper spray. She'd have her heart attack later.

She took another step and then another, until she was right outside the door. Then, without giving herself time to think, she shoved it all the way open and stood there staring inside.

At first glance, nothing was amiss. She looked around, relieved that nobody was inside. At least, not anyone willing to show themselves. Everything seemed to be where she'd left it. Everything—

And that's when she saw it. The dresser that she'd been working on, the one she'd so painstakingly stripped and refinished, had something dripping down the side. Her nostrils prickled with the tangy smell of fresh paint.

Gripping the Mace, she looked around again. She was alone. She let her gaze settle on the dresser again and stepped forward slowly. A gallon of white paint, paint that she kept securely on the shelf above, had fallen onto the dresser. It had pooled there in a sticky lake before running in long fingers down the side. It glistened underneath the shop lights. The dresser had been in the final stages of drying, it had been so pretty, one of Summer's favorite pieces so far. Stripping it had taken a long time, and now she'd have to start all over. The sight of the paint seeping into the lovely, natural wood made her sick.

She looked up at the shelf where the paint can had been. She'd never leave something open like that. Also, a gallon of paint didn't just teeter on the edge of a shelf and fall over on its own. Someone had been in here. But she realized with a pang that it would be impossible to prove. It would look like this was an accident—something careless that she'd let happen herself, when she knew damn well she hadn't.

She pulled her phone from her back pocket and took a quick picture of the dresser before backing out of the shop and locking the door behind her. She'd send a picture to Chief Martinez when she got to Beau's. But right now she just wanted to get as far away as possible. Eric had been here, or was *still* here, and she no longer felt even a modicum of safety on her property.

Clutching her bag to her chest, she jogged to her truck in the darkness. Her heart felt like it was going to slam right out of her chest. She'd been absolutely right when she'd thought things with Eric were coming to a head.

She knew that now beyond a shadow of a doubt.

Chapter Thirteen

Beau handed Summer a steaming mug of vanilla chai and then sat down beside her. The apartment was quiet, everyone else had gone to bed. Cora, Poppy and Mary were sharing a bedroom so Summer could have her own, something that she'd protested greatly about, but the decision had already been made. His cousins wanted her to be as comfortable as possible, and Mary was thrilled to have her staying with them—she didn't care where she slept.

Beau watched as she took a sip of her tea and then leaned back on the couch, looking tired. She'd told him about the paint incident as soon as she'd walked through the door, as well as the fact that she'd already sent pictures to the police. The camera she'd set up outside her shop had been tampered with. This whole thing was getting out of control. He wasn't sure how he was going to convince her to stay here after her birthday, but he'd have to try.

She took another sip from her mug then cupped it in her lap with both hands. She looked like she was drawing comfort from its warmth.

"I'm glad you're here," he said.

She smiled, but he could see the worry line between her brows, even in the dim light of the living room.

"I'm glad I'm here, too. I just wish you'd let me sleep on a cot or something. I feel bad."

"You saw the look on Mary's face when you got here. You're making her entire summer by staying here. Don't feel bad."

Summer laughed. "I've never made anyone's summer before."

"I don't know. You're making mine pretty nice."

She gazed back at him. Her hair was hanging loose past her shoulders tonight. He'd just said that she'd made his summer *nice.* It wasn't true. She'd made this one of the best summers he'd ever had, and that had taken him by surprise. It had happened so fast, he'd barely had time to register it, let alone figure out how he felt about it. All he knew was that, like he'd said, he was glad she was there. He didn't want her anywhere else but sitting close to him. Close enough to touch. Close enough to kiss.

"When you look at me like that, I can almost imagine you staying." She'd said it with her lips tilted, two small, familiar dimples at the corners. But her eyes were sad. There was an undeniable look in them that said she didn't trust this. Not really. Why would she? Beau didn't trust it, either. Nothing in his life had ever been a sure thing. There'd never been a promise of anything, and that was because he hadn't committed to anything except his career.

Now… He thought he'd known what he'd wanted. What he'd always wanted, but the depth of the sorrow in those eyes was enough to make him question everything. And that wasn't a comfortable place to be.

He leaned away from her, almost as if he could lean away from his feelings at the same time. He'd known the second that Summer had walked back into his life that this could happen, and it had. She'd known it, too. And now, here they were. On the cusp of saying good-bye. Again.

"I know you're not going to stay, Beau," she said. "We don't have to argue about it, or have a big, long discussion. We already knew how this was going to end before it started, right?"

Behind the sadness in her eyes was a steeliness that had been born of pain and heartbreak. She might be sad about the thought of him leaving, but she wasn't going to be devastated again. She was stronger than that.

"You're right," he said. "We did."

"You know, I've been thinking…"

"About?"

"About this. About us."

Us. The way that sounded made his gut tighten.

"It's not too late to avoid the fallout, Beau," she said evenly. "I mean I know what I said. That we can just take things as they come, but is that really the best thing? When we both know how that fallout could feel?"

He felt the muscles in his jaw harden. "Pretty bad."

"Right."

"So what are you saying? We stop this? Whatever it is?"

"That's what I'm saying. I mean we're both adults. We're not kids who don't know what we're doing anymore. It seems like the smartest thing…"

"Well. I've never been particularly smart." He smiled but the truth was she was absolutely right. Putting the brakes on would be best for them both. But then he thought about not being able to reach for her like he was dying to and, God help him, he didn't know if he had the willpower to walk away before he did any more damage.

She smiled, too, and looked down at the mug of tea in her hands. "I think you know how I feel about you, Beau. I've been trying hard not to feel that way again, but…well. You know."

"I know," he said.

"But you're leaving again. Right?"

He swallowed and his throat felt tight. It was a significant question. But, really, it was the answer that was truly significant. That could be life-altering, if he let it be.

"Yes," he said, his voice low.

She nodded, her expression a perfect mask. She was going to protect herself. And she absolutely should protect herself from him.

"Then this is definitely what's right," she said. "What's smartest."

"Yes."

"So… Business partners only."

"Okay. Business partners only." He hated how that sounded. What he wanted—what he *really* wanted but would never admit to—was something else. He wanted to kiss her again. But it was more than that. It was the desire to have her back in his life, back not just for a few weeks or months, but back to stay. He wondered how it would feel, having Summer to wake up to in the morning. He wondered if he could ever have a life like that. He could, if he wanted it badly enough. But would it last? Could they build something new, something that would stand the test of time?

He slapped his knees and stood. Then walked around the couch to look out the window at the fishing boats in the harbor, their lights like low-hanging stars over the dark water.

He scrubbed his hands through his hair, ignoring the stiffness in his shoulder, then clasped the back of his neck, and stared outside.

"What is it?" Summer asked from behind him. "What's wrong?"

"Business partners..." He said it under his breath like he was trying it out for size.

It didn't fit.

"Beau?"

Shaking his head, he closed his eyes for a second, trying for some clarity that wouldn't come. When had she become something that he felt he couldn't do without? He hadn't even had a chance to get back to pro fishing yet. How was he going to feel when that was part of the equation again?

"You're right," he said. "I know you are. And it makes sense." He turned around and let his gaze lock with hers. A familiar heat pulsed between them. "But here's the thing. I don't want to be just business partners with you. And that's what's frustrating the hell out of me because, up until now, I had my life planned out. No complications. No responsibility to anything other than my career. I've always tried to steer clear of anything that would remind me of my mom and dad's shitshow of a marriage. All those things felt like the kiss of death for me."

She watched him, breathing shallowly. He could see the soft rise and fall of her chest from where he stood.

"Was that what I was for you?" she asked. "The kiss of death?"

"For fishing professionally? Absolutely. I knew if we stayed together, it wouldn't have worked."

"Fishing? Or our relationship?"

"Both. Fishing takes everything that I have."

"I don't believe that. You've got more to give than that, I can see it now. You just never trusted yourself to do it."

It was truer than she knew.

"I don't think it ever had anything to do with fishing, Beau," she said quietly.

He felt himself tense. She stood and walked slowly up to him. He didn't think she'd ever looked lovelier. He wanted to take her face in his hands and lean close to feel her breath on his lips. He wanted to pick her up and carry her to the bedroom, feeling her heat and her curves and her weight in his arms. He wanted to lay her down on the bed and kiss the long, graceful column of her neck. And, most of all, he wanted to wake up beside her. That's what he wanted more than anything.

"It's okay, you know," she said.

"What's okay?"

"It's okay to be scared. That's normal when you have something worth losing. And I think what we had was special. Losing it changed me in ways that I'm still trying to figure out. I'm still trying to get over you." She gave him a bittersweet smile. "I'm not sure I ever will."

He stared down at her, his heart beating steadily, his stomach twisting with the need to have what he knew he couldn't. What he'd spent years convincing himself he didn't need.

"Sometimes I'm sorry we ever met," he said. His voice was gravelly. It felt strange, and sounded even stranger, because he was finally, finally telling her the truth. "Because I think about you all the time. I think about how things were with us, and I think about what they could have been, and you're absolutely right. I'm scared, and pissed, and I don't know how not to be those things, because if I let them go, I'm afraid part of myself will go with them."

"That makes you human."

"I want to be able to promise you things."

"I know."

"I want to be someone you can trust."

"I know that, too." Her eyes grew glassy. "I wish we'd talked like this back then. I wish..."

"I wish a lot of things."

"We're a hot mess."

"Right?" He felt his mouth tilt in that way that his grandpa used to call his trademark. *If we only knew what you were thinking, kid*, he'd say. And Beau would smile more. He wondered what his grandfather would think about all of this. What he would say to Beau about Summer. He'd always had such good advice, not that Beau took it. His family had learned early on that he was pretty much going to do what he wanted, but that had never stopped them from trying to get him to listen.

He took a deep breath. What he would give for some wisdom from his grandfather right then. To hear that deep, rough voice, and the laugh that had been such a comfort in dark times. But the truth was, he knew what his grandpa would say. Earl Sawyer had always led with his heart and he'd tried to instill that in his grandchildren as well. Walking away from Summer again wouldn't be leading with anything but fear.

"I guess we could be business partners with benefits," she said. "There's always that."

"Speaking of a hot mess."

"Asking for trouble, right?"

"Slightly."

"So we're right back where we started."

He leaned closer at that. Looking down at her mouth, her lips, the freckles across her nose.

"Not a terrible place to be," he said quietly.

"No, not so terrible."

And then he kissed her. Breaking all their rules at once.

Summer didn't think she'd ever had a better birthday. Well, her seventh birthday had been pretty great. Her mother had borrowed an old film projector from one of her friends and had brought *Black Beauty* home on a big metal reel, showing it in their darkened family room with popcorn and homemade cupcakes. That birthday party had been epic. But this birthday... This birthday was pretty close to eclipsing that one. And if anyone had asked her before if that would've even been possible, Summer would have said absolutely not.

But here she was. Sitting on a small, chartered sailboat in Christmas Bay's moonlit harbor, drinking champagne with a man she'd been in love with since college. Watching the occasional fireworks explode in the sky, colorful sparks falling down like rain. She couldn't think of how it could get much better than this. Even *Black Beauty* had trouble competing.

Beau leaned back on the cushioned bench on the bow of the graceful little boat, which was named *Pacific Serendipity.* A lovely name for a lovely night, as far as

Summer was concerned. He took a sip of his champagne and then smiled over at her. She smiled back, her heart thumping against her breastbone. The salty sea air was chilly coming off the water, and she shivered. Yet inside she felt warm and fluttery. The boat's gentle rocking lulling her into what she knew was a false sense of security.

She took a sip of her own champagne, feeling the bubbles tickle her tongue, her throat, her nose. She looked up at the clear star-speckled sky and licked her lips, wondering when Beau's shoulder would be healed enough to fish professionally again. When he would walk out of her life for good. Because that was going to happen. It wasn't a matter of if, it was a matter of when. The logical part of her brain told her this. But as she sat there, the water lapping at the sides of the boat, she pushed that thought away. It was easy to let herself believe that maybe, just maybe, he might end up staying. Or he might end up wanting to have a long-distance relationship while he was away, something he hadn't even considered before.

It was easy to let herself go to these places because of the way he'd looked at her just now. He'd changed since that first day in Earl's Antiques. There was no doubt he had. But the question was, How much? How much was he going to let his guard down with her? How much was he going to let himself love and be loved? She still didn't know.

"You are absolutely gorgeous," he said quietly. "You know that, right?"

"Well, I've never thought of myself as gorgeous." She leaned back against the cushion and brought her feet up underneath her. "But a girl never gets tired of hearing things like that."

"I should've told you more often. Every chance I got. Maybe then you'd believe it now."

She felt her face warm. The more he talked to her like this, the deeper she fell. The more afraid she got. And the more she wanted to push all the red flags far, far away.

"You're a charmer, Beau," she said. "And you outdid yourself with this boat. With this birthday dinner."

"You only turn thirty once. It needed to be special."

"It was very special. Thank you."

"You're welcome."

"I'm not sure how I'm going to go back to reality after this," she said. But she needed to. She needed to get a grip on things before he ended up leaving, because she most definitely didn't have a grip on them now.

"I'm really glad you decided to stay with us for a while."

"Me too."

"I know the plan was for you to go after your birthday if things calmed down. But I think you should stay a little longer. Give it some time. I'm not crazy about the idea of you going back to your place by yourself."

Neither was she. Regardless, she couldn't stay with Beau forever, and things with Eric *had* calmed down. He hadn't contacted her in days, and Beau had been out to her place to check on things since she'd left, and nothing had seemed out of place. There was no way to tell for sure, but maybe he'd decided to leave her alone. Either way, she was going to have to deal with this. She had to go back to her house, she had to face it head-on. Running away wouldn't accomplish anything.

"I'll be okay," she said. "I will. I've got the cameras

working again, and if anything else happens, it's just more evidence to build a case against him."

"That doesn't make me feel better."

"I know. But what else can we do?"

"You can stay with us for a few more days. Just to ease my mind a little."

"Your family is probably sick of me by now."

"You know that's not true. Mary thinks you're the best thing since sliced bread. Roo follows you around like you own the place. My cousins adore you. So you'd be doing us a solid by sticking around."

She laughed, taking another sip of her champagne. "How about you?" she said, lowering the glass again. "I'm not cramping your bachelor style?"

"I don't know what I am anymore, but bachelor doesn't seem to fit."

She didn't want to let her heart skip at that. But it did anyway. It was so hard not to read into everything he said, all the sweet things he did, even though she knew she absolutely shouldn't.

"Well, you're single," she said. "At least officially."

He watched her, the moonlight playing over his face. He wore a white-collared shirt tonight and beige khakis. He was clean-shaven, but his hair was a little shaggy at the neckline. It was sun-bleached at the ends, and his skin was a deep golden brown. He'd hadn't been fishing competitively, of course, but he'd stayed active outdoors since moving back to Christmas Bay, hiking and running after they closed the shop at night. He was sexier than ever. Gone was that sharp look in his eyes, replaced by something softer and more relaxed. She liked to think she was partly to thank for that, but she knew him being with his family was having a profound effect. He wasn't alone anymore. Whether that had been the plan or not, it had ended up doing things for Beau that she wasn't sure he'd even realized yet.

"I feel like I'm kind of spoken for," he said.

Again, she had to work not to let that carry her away. He had feelings for her. That was obvious. He'd told her so. But that didn't mean they were going to have a happily-ever-after or anything. What it meant was that Summer was putting herself in a precarious position. One that her parents had warned her about. One that would end up breaking her heart again. Still, the words settled over her like a warm blanket, giving her a dangerous kind of hope that was like walking a high wire. One misstep and she was going to fall.

She didn't answer him. Because there was nothing left to say. She wasn't sure what she was going to do when the time came to choose between loving Beau and protecting herself, but, like Eric, she was going to have to face it sooner rather than later.

"Stay with us?" he asked again, this time lower. "Just for a few more days."

This time, she gave him a small smile. Then nodded. "Okay. For a few more days."

Chapter Fourteen

Beau hung up the phone and stared straight ahead. His blood was cold, his brain stuck on what Cast's representative had just said. *We have to pull your sponsorship, Beau. I'm so sorry.*

Poppy had been working on a display a few yards away, but had probably heard everything, since she'd set her armful of trinkets down and was staring at him now.

"Beau?" she asked. "Are you alright?"

He blinked at her. Furious. Not at her, of course, but he knew that anyone who got in his way right then would take the brunt of his anger.

"I'm fine."

"Do you want to talk about it?"

Without answering, he got up and headed toward the front door. Not knowing where he was going but needing to escape the antique shop where the walls felt like they were closing in.

He pushed the door open, standing aside for a couple of women who smiled and walked inside. And then he jammed his hands in his pockets and headed down the sidewalk with the salty breeze blowing against his skin. Cooling it a little. Calming him enough that he didn't actually punch something like he really wanted to.

He couldn't blame Cast for pulling his sponsorship. He wasn't fishing right now. It made sense. Still, that didn't soften the blow. It felt like being hit in the chest with a mallet and left struggling to breathe. He'd worked his ass for this sponsorship. It had taken him so damn long to get to this point, to be good enough where he could make a decent living doing what he loved. And now, with one phone call, it was over. Yes, he could try to work his way back. But who knew how long it would take to prove himself again? And the bigger question was, would his shoulder be up to it?

Scowling at the sidewalk, he kicked at a pebble. His mood was dark, but at the same time, he knew this was how life went. Sometimes you got lucky. Sometimes your luck ran out. He knew he should consider himself fortunate that Cast had stuck with him for as long as they had. Still, he couldn't seem to muster the Glass Half Full motto that his grandfather had always been so good at. Right now, he felt angry. He felt sad. He felt stressed, because he knew that if he wanted any chance at getting his sponsorship back, he had to get back on the water.

As tourists passed by on the sidewalk, he thought of Summer and how, without meaning to, he'd started leading her to believe that he might be staying. Settling here, or at least being open to having a long-distance relationship. Had he said those exact words? No, but he hadn't really needed to. He'd implied it by asking her to stay with him. By taking her out on that boat for her birthday. By giving her champagne and telling her how pretty she was. By kissing her… All things that had come from his heart. But it didn't matter now. They were things that implied he was ready for more, and he'd done them anyway.

Now, with a two-minute phone call, he was faced with the reality he'd been so willing to push away in favor of living in a fantasy world where he'd be able to get back to his career at his leisure. When he was good and ready. But that wasn't how it worked, and he was going to have to hustle, whether he was ready or not. Whether his shoulder was ready or not. And whether he was ready to walk away from Summer again.

He scrubbed a hand through his hair as mottled seagulls bobbed and bickered overhead. Had that been his intention all along? Lead her on and then walk away? He didn't like to think it was, but he'd known his goal had never wavered. He'd always planned on going back to sportfishing, or at least giving it his best shot. And that meant he'd be hurting Summer all over again. And hurting his cousins, who were hoping he'd stay longer than just the year their grandfather had asked for in his will.

Swallowing hard, he looked out over the historic red-brick buildings on Main Street, to Cape Longing beyond. From here, he could see the iconic yellow Victorian house that had once belonged to Frances O'Hara. Her foster daughter and son-in-law owned it now and, in the summers, they used it for a camp for disadvantaged kids. The news in Portland had done a piece on it recently. The entire town had been so proud. Beau had been proud, too. These were the things that had started mattering to him over the last few months. Slowly but surely, he'd developed a sense of home again. A sense of belonging that he hadn't felt in a very long time. And then there was Summer...

He'd let himself love her again. But everyone knew he wasn't the kind of guy to stay in one place for very long. His cousins knew that—even though they'd been hoping for one thing, they'd surely expected something else. And Summer knew it, too. Still, the thought of leaving them turned his stomach. Broke his heart. It was a new feeling for him. He'd always prided himself on being so pragmatic and realistic. And if he'd been accused of being a little callous too...well, then, that wasn't such a bad thing, was it?

He wasn't sure when he'd started changing, but he knew one thing for sure. If he was going to fish professionally again, he would have to put the work in to get back to where he'd been before.

And that meant leaving Christmas Bay.

Summer stepped away from the open window over the sink, the sheer white curtains billowing in the breeze. She'd bought a flat of colorful petunias and had spent the afternoon planting them in pots of various sizes and placing them on the apartment's windowsills. It was a small gesture, but she'd wanted to do something nice for Beau and his cousins for having her. It had been the nicest week, and she'd felt the most relaxed, happy and safe that she had in a long time. The flowers were the least she could do.

Crossing her arms over her chest, she smiled at their velvety petals. *Happy...* That was the word that kept coming back again and again. Despite being hesitant to stay there, feeling like she'd be putting everyone out, she'd ended up feeling welcome. They'd all been so nice. And Beau had been a friend to her when she'd needed one most. So much so, that she was beginning to think that trying for some kind of relationship might not be so crazy after all. With every day that passed, he'd shown her how much he'd grown since those college days. He was finally acting like someone with something to lose. And not just the sport he loved so much.

From downstairs came the faint sound of voices. She'd been there long enough to know it wasn't unusual to hear people downstairs, it was a business after all, and there was a lot of activity down there during the day. But something about the way these voices clashed, elevated, sharp, made her step a little closer to the vent where the echo traveled more easily through the old building.

It sounded like Beau and Poppy, who were downstairs working, while Cora watched a movie with Mary in the bedroom. They were arguing. But why? What in the world could they be arguing about?

And then, like a knife to the belly, she heard her name. And there was an inflection at the end, like a question.

Summer leaned away from the vent. Maybe she'd been wrong, maybe she had overstayed her welcome. Suddenly, she was uncomfortable in her own skin. If her name had come up during an argument, she wanted to know why. Maybe she could help somehow. Of course, there was always the possibility that going down there might just make it worse…

And then she heard her name again. This time from Beau. This time his voice was booming, and she knew that in order for him to sound this upset, something must have happened between now and when she'd seen him that morning. She also knew there weren't any customers in the shop. There couldn't be with all this yelling going on.

Without giving herself time to change her mind, she headed down the narrow staircase that led to the shop.

The voices that had been muffled before were now sharp as blades, scraping against each other.

"Somebody needs to say this to you," Poppy said. "Somebody needs to try and get you to see what you're doing."

"And what am I doing?"

"Isn't it obvious by now, Beau? You're running away."

"I'm trying to get my life back."

"Your life is here, your family is here. And Summer is here."

"You knew this was the deal. You knew I'd be leaving again."

"There's a difference between leaving and cutting all ties. You just said this is for good, so why should we think you'll be coming back at all? You said there's nothing between you and Summer, and you know there is. *She* believes there is."

"I can't help that."

Summer stood there on the bottom step. She could see them now. They were behind the counter, next to the cash register. And she'd been right, the shop was empty. In fact, someone had hung the Closed sign in the window.

She realized she was shaking. Not five minutes ago, she'd been thinking about the possibility of a relationship with Beau. A *relationship.* And now, here she was, trying not to cry. Trying hard to be more furious at him than at herself for stepping right into the quicksand that was Beau Evers. Hadn't she known this was how it was going to be? She'd known it, and she'd been so careless anyway.

She must've made a sound because they both looked over at the same time. The expression on Poppy's face was one of sadness. She felt sorry for Summer; it was obvious, from one woman to another. Maybe Poppy, at some point, had been where Summer was now—in love with a man who was destined to be just out of her reach.

But the expression on Beau's face was what made Summer's breath catch in her throat. He looked exactly—*exactly*—like he had that day in college. When he'd broken up with her in the fall, with the leaves falling all around them. He looked so far away, like he'd managed to reach inside his chest and switch his heart to the off position.

She stared at him and he stared back.

"How long have you been standing there?" he asked, his voice low.

"Long enough. I heard you from upstairs."

Poppy's face colored. "I'm sorry, Summer."

"You have nothing to be sorry for."

Poppy looked from Summer to Beau. "Well," she said. "I'm going to go walk Roo."

Without another word, she brushed by Summer with a quick squeeze of her arm.

And then she was gone and they were alone, and to Summer, it felt like the entire room had been sucked free of oxygen.

Beau watched her, probably expecting her to start

yelling at him. Accusing him of who knew what. But honestly, she didn't have the words. She was just tired. And her heart ached from somewhere so deep that it felt like her body had been turned inside out. How had she ever let herself believe it could end any other way? She thought she'd learned so much since their breakup and had come so far. But, in reality, she'd never let herself do the hardest work of all, which was letting him go completely.

Beau put his hands in his pockets and looked at the floor. The muscles in his forearms were flexed and tight. So was his jaw. She could see it bunching from where she stood.

"Cast pulled my sponsorship," he said evenly.

She watched him, her stomach sinking. Despite everything, despite the anger and the pain and the fatigue, she felt his words to her core. She knew what this sponsorship meant to him. It was his career, his dream, what he'd worked so hard for. She didn't know what he was going to do without it, how he'd move forward, but it was obvious what he was going through right now.

"I'm sorry, Beau."

"Yeah, well..." Still, he didn't look at her. The only time she'd ever seen him fight this much emotion was when he'd broken up with her. He hadn't cried, but he'd been close. There had been a lot of things wrong with their relationship back then, but love hadn't been one of them. She'd always known he'd loved her, but sometimes love wasn't enough.

"Your shoulder is healing," she said. "You'll get it back."

"I don't know. I'm going to have to work twice as

hard. And I'm not sure if the strength will ever be where it was."

"If anyone can do it, you can."

His gaze settled on hers and his eyes were red-rimmed. "I never should've come back. It was a mistake."

She stiffened. Was he talking about coming back to town? Or coming back and getting involved with her again?

"I don't think my grandpa understood what he was asking," he continued. "I just don't."

"You came back to your family, Beau. That was a good thing."

He shook his head. "I'm going to hurt them. I'm going to hurt you, and I'm not sure how I let that happen."

"So you're leaving." It wasn't a question. It hadn't been for a long time.

"Yes."

"When?"

"Soon. I have some money in savings. I can live on that for a while. But I need to be where the tournaments are."

She bit the inside of her lip. Fishing was taking him again. Always the tournaments. Always the travel. Always the turning away from the people who loved him. The severing of ties was a theme in his life. And that made her sad for all of them.

"It sounds like you've got it all worked out," she said, struggling to keep her voice from breaking. "Maybe you just weren't meant to stay in one place for too long."

What she didn't say was, *Maybe you aren't meant to have a home*. But that sounded too dark and she wasn't sure she believed it anyway. Really, she thought he'd find his way back here again. But by then she'd be gone. Gone from his life for good.

The expression on his face said so many things. Mostly, he just looked resigned. Resigned to the fate of being alone. Of not getting attached, of not making the same mistakes his parents had made. She remembered him telling her once that it had been miserable watching their marriage fall apart. He'd felt caught in the middle as a boy, like loving one of them was being disloyal to the other one. Until he'd just pushed them both away, not knowing what else to do. That had been years ago. His pain had only grown deeper with age, his boyhood confusion a chasm that nobody was meant to cross. That was by design. It was so clear to her now, and it broke her heart.

"I wish I could say things would work long distance," he said. "But I don't know when I could make it back, how often..."

She shook her head. "Don't."

"I'm just saying—"

"Don't, Beau. I'm not blaming you, I knew this would probably happen. Even if I was trying to convince myself of something else. But don't try to tell me that you *wish* you could make it work, because we both know you could if you really wanted to. And that's okay. Now, I know. Now, I know for sure, and that's what I needed to finally be able to move on."

He rubbed his temple. Silence settled between them. The shop was so quiet that Summer felt like she could hear the blood flowing through her veins. She'd managed not to cry, which she thought was pretty amazing since she'd felt the ache of tears at the back of her throat for the last five minutes now.

Beau closed his eyes for a second, those beautiful blue eyes that any woman would have trouble not losing herself in. Summer had been lost for a while, and then she'd found herself, and then she'd gotten lost again. This time, though, she wasn't going to be led astray. She was going to harden her heart and she was going to get down to work, make her business a success. And someday, maybe she'd be like Beau—Teflon. A person who wouldn't let anyone or anything stick. Ever.

The thought made her swallow hard. Her throat ached but she wasn't going to let it show. Suddenly, she was desperate to get back to her little house. Even with the possibility of Eric somewhere close by, the thought of that was better than the thought of one more second there, swallowing tears that were threatening to choke her where she stood.

"I'm sorry," he said quietly. "I wish I could be another kind of man for you."

She pressed her lips together to keep herself from answering too quickly. Because she wasn't at all sure that her voice wouldn't break after all. That she wouldn't break. She had to consciously will herself to stay silent or risk telling him she'd wait for him, and she wasn't going to do that to herself.

She forced her shoulders back and took a deep breath. This was goodbye.

"I love you, Beau," she said.

He watched her. Those lovely eyes were a vast ocean, uncharted territory, deep and cool and wide. And then he took a step toward her and reached his hand out. To do what? To pull her close? To hold her one last time? To kiss her goodbye?

It didn't matter. She wasn't going to let herself go to him again. She *did* love him, and she wanted him to know that. But she would not go to him again.

She took a step back and he froze, recognizing it for what it was—a protective measure.

"Good luck," she said. "I want the best for you. I always have. You're a special person, but you're not *my* person. Not anymore."

She could tell he believed her. That this was it, finally. They'd danced around this for years, even though they'd only been back in each other's orbit for part of the summer. The finality of it was enough to make her knees weak.

Before she could start swaying, which she absolutely knew she would if she stood there another second longer, she turned and walked back up the stairs. To say goodbye to his cousins and to Mary. To gather her things and her courage, and leave this place where she'd felt more like herself over these few short days than she had, maybe ever.

She would start over. She'd be okay.

She kept repeating that in her head until she reached the door at the top of the staircase and pushed it open. Mary was sitting on the couch. And when she looked up and saw Summer walk in, she ran to give her a hug.

It was exactly what Summer needed. As she wrapped her arms around the girl, whose body was so angular against hers, she reminded herself again that she was going to be okay.

There was a time before Beau. And there would be a time after him, too.

* * *

The water was still today. Quiet. Even the birds in the evergreens surrounding the fishing hole were silent, something that was almost never the case. It was as if Mother Nature herself wanted Beau to be able to clear his head. Clear his heart of all the things that had been weighing him down and be free of them once and for all.

He sat there, on the rock outcropping that he and Summer had jumped off of just a few short weeks ago, and stared out over the water to the meadow beyond. He'd thought when this moment came that he'd be ready. That he'd be able to tell Summer goodbye, that it had been nice spending some time together. In his mind, he'd always pictured himself telling her he had to get back to his career—reminding her that his time in Christmas Bay had been temporary, finite. She'd be a little sad, and so would he, but in the end it would all work out and they'd move on from each other neatly. With no lingering emotion, and certainly no pain to get through.

But he'd been wrong about all of it, of course. He'd been an idiot. Of course, it would be messy. Of course, there would be pain. And the pain was significant. It was a physical ache that hadn't left him since Summer had disappeared up the stairs that day to pack her things. It had settled inside Beau's bones the second she'd told him that she loved him. He hadn't been able to sleep since—tossing and turning, and getting up well before dawn to go running every morning. He'd hoped that tiring his body out would mean tiring his mind out, too. That he'd stop thinking about her so much, stop obsessing over that last day together. But nothing worked.

He sat there, his shoulders tense, his back tense. He

stared at the meadow grass moving in the breeze. Hugging his knees, he rocked a little, unaware that he was doing it until the rock began biting into his backside. He shifted, his thoughts shifting, too.

Poppy and Cora would barely speak to him. And he knew it wasn't because he was going back to fishing, although that was partly it. Leaving was breaking his promise to stay and help them run the shop for a year. As it stood now, he'd only been here close to six months. He fully intended to be back when he could, periodic weekends and holidays, but it wasn't the same. Just to be safe, he'd contacted their family attorney, and made sure that leaving wouldn't nullify their grandpa's will. He'd also told his cousins that he'd forfeit his share of the inheritance, and they'd said that was ridiculous, but they were still salty. But what had them *really* upset was the fact that he was leaving Summer again. He couldn't figure out if it was because they liked Summer so much or if they liked *him* with Summer. Probably a combination of the two. But either way, they'd forgive him eventually.

What he was most worried about was Mary, who'd run out of the room crying the day Summer had left. He hadn't been able to stop thinking about that, either. The knowledge that all this was happening just as she was grieving the loss of her dad. Even though Beau had promised her he'd be back to visit, he felt like he was abandoning her. And not just her—all of them. His family. And the woman he loved.

He hadn't been able to say it to Summer the day she'd gone home because he'd been still grappling with the reality of it himself. But with each passing hour, it was sinking in deeper and deeper. That knowledge, alongside the ache in his bones. He loved her. He'd never loved anyone else like he loved her, and probably never would.

Shifting again, he pushed himself up with his relatively good arm. Then stood, his knees popping. He felt old and worn out at thirty. But it wasn't his joints making him feel this way, it was his life in general. His lack of roots, his lack of ties, his lack of love. Just as he'd started cultivating those things in a meaningful way, he'd found himself turning his back on them again. He'd been spooked, scared off by a simple phone call about his sponsorship. Was it just an excuse? Was it just a way to be able to justify leaving the things behind that meant the most to him? He used to think sportfishing meant the most. But it was becoming painfully clear that he'd been the happiest when he hadn't been fishing, at least not professionally. He'd felt the most liberated this last month, the freest, the most peaceful—and that was ironic because he'd always thought his career was what had given him those things.

Now he was stuck between the life he'd thought he wanted and the life he'd been given. He stared down at the water and saw trout swimming below. It was a sight that never failed to stop his heart. He loved the feeling of reeling them in. Of pulling them out of the water, of holding their cool, slippery bodies in his hands. He thought about how it felt to let the littler ones go and watch them swim off, knowing they were going to get bigger and become a challenge for him later. He loved the ritual of it. He loved being so close to nature and the part of himself that was able to breathe a little easier in the natural world. Beau had always felt the most at home when he was fishing.

Until he'd come back to Christmas Bay.

He pulled his baseball cap low over his eyes as the sun sank further in the sky, reflecting off the water in bright yellow sparkles. He'd told Cora and Poppy that he'd be leaving by the end of the week. He wanted to help them get through the next round of inventory. And he wanted to ease Mary into the idea of him going. He'd found a tournament on the east coast that would be happening at the beginning of next month. If he hustled, he could be ready. Or, at least, as ready as he'd ever be. His shoulder felt strong, with the exception of some lingering stiffness in the mornings.

And all of that was good. It was great. Except that his heart wasn't in it. He couldn't shake the feeling that he was about to make a huge mistake.

With a sigh, he turned away from the fishing hole and away from the memory of Summer jumping in it. Away from the memory of the water droplets on her pale skin as she'd resurfaced. He'd kissed her that afternoon, and had only been thinking of himself, as usual. Of how much he'd wanted her and how much he'd wanted to taste those droplets on his tongue. The thought of kissing her again was suddenly so overwhelming that he had to shake his head, as if telling his heart to ease up a little. To let go.

But did he really want to let go? He kept asking himself that same question as he climbed inside his truck and started the engine. He yanked the sun visor down and took off his baseball cap to run his hand through his hair.

Did he want to let go? The answer had always been elusive, a fish darting just beneath the shimmering surface.

He just didn't know.

Chapter Fifteen

Summer sat on her porch swing and rocked back and forth, the gentle squeak reminding her of her childhood. Her parents' house had had a screened-in front porch and she used to curl up on the swing and read until it was time for bed. Her mother would call her inside and she'd always beg for just one more chapter. Those had been good days. Simpler days, when she hadn't realized how screwed up the world could be. How screwed up people could be. She'd just felt safe and loved and happy.

Now, as she pushed the swing with her bare feet skimming the porch, she wished she could go back there—back to when her heart had never been broken. Back to where feeling safe and loved was the default and her days were spent inside her own vividly colorful imagination where nothing could hurt her.

She watched as the sun sank low in the horizon, turning the sky a marigold orange. She thought about calling Angie back, since her friend had called earlier, but Summer had been feeding Tank, who seemed happy to be home. At least, that's what his appetite would indicate.

But she hesitated to pick up the phone because she knew Angie would want to know what was happening with Beau and Summer just couldn't go there yet. Her heart had been hurting ever since leaving the apartment above the antique shop. She'd driven home with tears streaming down her face and it had taken all her willpower to stop crying long enough to call Dr. Poet and tell him she was back.

The tears had finally eased up, thank goodness, but the pain remained. She thought she'd been prepared for Beau, but she hadn't been prepared at all. She just hadn't. She felt naïve and silly, and too much like that girl she'd been in college for comfort.

Now it was time to pick up the pieces and move on. This time for good.

At least there'd been no sign of Eric since she'd been home. She'd been in contact with Chief Martinez and his officers had been driving by regularly, making themselves known and visible, which made her feel better. She'd also installed floodlights with motion sensors around the house and another camera in back of the shop. This was about all she could reasonably do, aside from sleeping with a bazooka underneath her pillow.

She smiled at the image but felt it fade on her lips at the next thought she had, which was of Beau. Thoughts of Beau were plentiful. Actually, they were never-ending, one after the other, but at least she was able to power through them now, which was more than she could say a few days ago when thinking of him made her want to curl into the fetal position and sob.

There was something about how it had ended this time that was especially hard to accept. And that was because, despite everything, she'd really let herself believe there could be a future with him. It hurt to realize she'd been so wrong. That she'd once again chosen not to see the warning signs because of how she felt about him. He wasn't the only one she was disappointed in. She was disappointed in herself, too.

Beside her on the swing, her phone chimed with a new text. Probably Angie wanting to talk. Summer wasn't going to be able to hold her off much longer.

With a sigh, she reached over and swiped her iPhone open. But it wasn't a text from her best friend. It was a text from Beau.

Her heart slowed to a laborious thump as she stared down at it.

I keep thinking about you.

She swallowed hard. It didn't matter if he was thinking about her, she wasn't going to respond. She wasn't going to get pulled back in. He was leaving, and she was devastated, and the only way to make it better was to distance herself from him.

She stood, tucking her phone into her pocket. She'd go inside and lock the doors and pour herself a glass of wine. And then she'd call Angie and she'd let her best friend remind her of all the reasons why it was good to be free of Beau Evers once and for all.

She just hoped she'd have enough sense to listen this time.

"Uncle Beau."

"Hmm?"

"I asked when you'll be back to visit. Mom said you might try to be home for Labor Day, before I go back to school."

Beau set his phone down, farther away this time. Maybe that would keep him from checking it every five minutes. It was pretty obvious Summer wasn't going to text back. And could he blame her? Still, he hated the finality of it. He hated how much he wanted to hear from her again and how this whole damn thing was his own fault. And even if he was having second thoughts, she probably wouldn't—wisely—have anything to do with him.

"Uncle Beau?"

"Yes, honey. Sorry."

Mary was leaning against the antique shop front counter. She was wearing her roller skates and had her helmet and knee and elbow pads on, something that Cora now insisted she wear since her last fall had nearly ended with stitches.

"Labor Day," Mary repeated. "Will you be back before then?" She had a tone. It was the tone kids used to speak to adults when they were trying not to show how exasperating they thought they were. Beau recognized it because he remembered using it himself when he was her age.

"Yes," he said. "I'll be back before you start school. I promise."

"I wish you weren't going at all," Mary muttered.

He walked around the counter and wrapped her in a hug. She was getting so tall. Ready to start middle school, such a big deal for a kid her age. The guilt he had about leaving her was starting to eat at him. It was leaving a Mary-sized hole right in his heart.

"I'm sorry," he said.

"You *could* stay, you know."

"And do what?"

"Run the shop with Mom and Aunt Poppy."

"I was never supposed to stay forever, Mary."

"But I was hoping you'd like it."

"I do like it."

"Then why don't you stay?"

How was he supposed to answer that? Even he didn't think his reasons were as clear as they'd been before. It was starting to feel like the main motive for leaving was a fear of staying, not a passion for adventure, or for the sport, or for anything else. And that was a hard thing to say out loud, a hard thing for him to admit to.

So he kept quiet and just hugged her tighter.

When he let go and stepped back, he felt Roo leaning against his leg. She'd sidled up to him without a sound, something she was pretty good at for being as big as she was.

"See?" Mary said. "Roo doesn't want you to go, either."

"Roo just likes me because I feed her."

"We all feed her. You're her favorite."

"No, you're her favorite."

"We're *both* her favorite."

"Hey!" Poppy said, walking over. "You said I was her favorite a few days ago."

Mary smiled, that adorable preteen smile, with freckles to boot. "Well, you know. She loves us all pretty much the same."

"Uh-huh."

Mary pushed away from the counter and skated into the back room with Roo trotting along behind, the dog's nails clicking on the hardwood floor.

"See what you'll be missing?" Poppy asked, watching them go.

"I already feel bad enough."

His cousin looked over at him. "So what does that tell you?"

"That I've developed an annoying conscience?"

"Or maybe you just like it here."

Beau sighed. It wasn't that easy. Or maybe it was.

"I'm just saying," she went on. "You should think it over before you pack up and leave us. And Summer. You might regret it, you know."

"So you've said."

"You know I'm right."

He did know she was right. He knew because that small biting feeling of regret was becoming sharp and recognizable in his gut. He'd been having unsettling dreams about leaving—dreams about his cousins, his family, and waking up to a sick, heavy feeling in his heart. And he was dreaming of Summer, too. In his dreams, he kept trying to reach for her, but she was always just beyond his fingertips. Smiling, loving him. Getting farther and farther away. He didn't have to have a psychology degree to figure out what that meant. He was definitely having second thoughts. He was thinking about what it would be like to stay. To explore something beyond sportfishing, something that would allow him to form some real relationships, some lasting connections in his life.

So, yes. He was already regretting this decision, even though his bags were packed and he was just about ready to go.

But he wasn't gone yet. Maybe…just maybe…

He didn't finish that thought. He watched Poppy turn

and follow Mary and Roo into the back of the shop. Mary had made cookies an hour ago and had brought them down on a platter. He could smell their warm sugary scent from where he stood. It made him think of the day Summer had brought him cookies after his surgery. The day they'd argued and she'd left and he'd thought it would be the last time he'd see her.

Except it hadn't been the last time. He'd apologized and they'd moved forward, and they'd ended up falling for each other again. A foregone conclusion to everyone but him, it seemed. But it had happened and now he was finding himself at a crossroads. Go or stay. Stay or go. Going would require nothing more than leaning back into a lifelong habit. Doing what was easiest had always been Beau's default. Staying would require work. It would require change. And it would require faith, something that he'd never had much of. But that didn't mean it couldn't be done.

"Uncle Beau!" Mary called. "They're already cold!"

He smiled. "I'll be there in a second, kiddo."

He looked out the window of the antique shop to the sidewalk where tourists were strolling by, ever-present coffees in their hands. Bags slung over their shoulders. Wanderlust in their eyes. Once upon a time, Beau couldn't wait to leave Christmas Bay and its revolving door of people behind. But he'd come back. It hadn't been to stay, but he'd settled in just the same. And now he thought he'd miss the strangers who came in and out of his life on a daily basis. He'd miss his cousins who kept giving him relationship advice, as if he'd had one in the first place. He'd miss his niece who made cookies and roller-skated with abandon, and who was getting ready to step up to the edge of middle school, a yawning precipice of preteen angst.

And he'd miss his Summer. She'd become his when he wasn't looking. When he wasn't paying attention. She'd become someone he didn't want to leave. But more than that, she'd become someone he thought he might be able to have faith in.

Or maybe he was ready to have some faith in himself.

Maybe. Just maybe.

Summer looked down at the coffee table with her hands planted on her hips. She'd brought it home from someone's driveway just down the highway. It'd had a sad little sign taped to it that had been flapping in the breeze: Free to Good Home!

It was mid-century modern, her favorite. It also had water marks all over the maple wood, rings where people had set dewy drinks down without a coaster. It had loose, wobbly legs, one of them with a sizeable crack. But what Summer saw when she looked at it was a lovely diamond in the rough. It would sparkle when she was done with it. It would be a perfect piece for the mansion in Eugene, which was turning out to be the project of her heart. The furniture she'd been collecting and working on was an eclectic mix, no two pieces were quite the same. She hoped Betsy, the woman who owned the place, would be happy with them. But at this point, Summer thought she was happy enough for the both of them. She'd done the best work of her life on this collection, and she was proud of it.

She took a step back and looked over at the rest of the furniture under the soft shop lighting. It was dusk, another day slipping quietly into night. Another storm blowing in off the ocean, this most recent one beginning to huff and puff and rattle the old windowpanes with its bluster. She thought about Beau then, like she always did at this time of day. She knew why night brought on the loneliness, the longing. She wished she could have dinner with him, a glass of wine maybe, and talk about their day. She wished she could climb into bed next to him and have him hold her tight until she fell asleep. But more than anything, she wished she could wake up next to him and do it all over again.

She understood all that; she got the why of it. But it didn't make it any easier when thoughts of him made their way into her head, into her heart. They were a constant, painful bombardment that made it hard to sleep at all much less concentrate on work.

But somehow, some way, she'd found the wherewithal to do just that. She had a roomful of reminders that even though she was heartbroken, she could do hard things. This work was the best she'd ever done. And she thought she had Beau to thank for that. Maybe the distraction had done her good. It had come at the best possible time; when she'd needed to throw herself into something other than missing him. She'd directed her love at the furniture when she couldn't direct it at Beau anymore.

The wind pushed against the shop again and the walls creaked in protest. She walked over to the window and looked out at Tank's shed. Dark, surly clouds were building in the dusky sky and she knew it would rain soon. But her sweet goat was snug in his new bed of straw, looking unbothered by the current weather.

She bit her lip and turned away. She'd gotten some

solid work done today, and that was good. But she felt strange and couldn't understand why. Ever since coming back to her place after staying with the Sawyers, things with Eric had been quiet. Not a peep from him. She should've been confident that he was long gone by now, but instead she felt the opposite. Like the longer she went without hearing from him, the surer she was that he was still out there. Still watching her from afar.

The wind moaned around the shop and the lights flickered. Shivering, she took out her phone and brought up the security camera app. It was habit; she viewed it regularly now. But tonight she felt the need to double-check. It was probably the storm—the creaking and popping of the old shop, the impending rain and darkness—that was making her jumpy. Still, she couldn't shake the feeling that something was off, and Chief Martinez had told her over and over again to trust her instincts.

She checked the images from the cameras one by one and saw nothing out of the ordinary in the grainy video. Just trees blowing in the wind. Her hanging plants swinging back and forth.

And then the lights flickered again.

She froze until they steadied once more. The odds that the electricity would go out tonight were pretty good. It wasn't unusual for the entire town of Christmas Bay to go dark during the stronger storms. Still, Summer hated when it happened and hated it even more now that she had a stalker she didn't necessarily feel was in her rear-view mirror yet.

With every flicker of the lights, with every gust of wind, Summer questioned why she'd chosen to live all the way out here by herself. In the morning, she knew those questions would fade along with the remnants of the storm, but right now they were very real, and very big.

Her phone dinged from her pocket and she pulled it out again. There on the screen was a simple, sweet text from Beau.

Storm will be bad. Let me know you're alright.

She stared at it, and her eyes filled with quick tears. It was the same kind of text he'd sent a few weeks ago—checking on her during the same kind of storm. She thought about all the things that had happened since then, all the ways that she'd lost herself to him.

She swallowed but the stubborn lump in her throat remained. How she wanted to give in to this. How she wanted to text him back, or better yet, ask him to come over, like he had before. This time she'd make them some dinner and they'd watch a movie if the lights stayed on long enough. And if they didn't, they could find other ways to entertain themselves.

But he wasn't her boyfriend. He wasn't even her friend at the moment, and asking him to come over was out of the question. At least as far as her heart was concerned. She was determined not to read anything into this. If she was going to get over Beau, she *couldn't* read anything into it. He might be blurring the line between caring about her and loving her, but she wasn't going to blur anything.

As she held the phone, looking down at it through tears, it dinged with another text.

I know you're trying to distance yourself, and I get it. But at least let me know you're okay?

Summer pulled in a deep breath, letting it saturate her lungs before releasing it again. It was a reasonable ask. She shouldn't leave him hanging when he was clearly worried. What she was most concerned about, though, was letting him back in. It would be so easy to do. But texting him back to put his mind at ease wouldn't hurt. Would it?

She clicked on the thread she'd shared with him for weeks, thinking about what to say. She didn't want to be too short but she didn't want to go into detail, either. All of a sudden, she felt like a teenager trying to negotiate the delicate task of communication while analyzing every word.

She licked her lips as another gust of wind made some tree branches slap against the windows. Or, at least, she thought they were tree branches…

She waited a second, listening. When she was sure, or reasonably sure, there wasn't anyone outside getting ready to murder her, she studied her phone again with a frown.

And that's when she heard it. Startling, she looked up. A tapping against the window across the shop. It was the exact same kind of tapping that she'd heard a few weeks ago when she'd ended up calling the police. When it had turned out to be nothing more than her overactive imagination.

Summer had felt so silly then and the last thing she wanted, or needed, was for that to happen again. She'd wait a minute or two. With any luck, it would turn out to be nothing, just like last time, and she'd go inside and lock up for the night.

She stood there, trying not to shake, but failing miserably. Her phone felt slippery in her hand and she thought about Beau, who was waiting for a reply. It would be so easy to tell him that she was spooked and that she'd love to see a friendly face right about now.

But she was stubborn and hurt, and she just couldn't let herself do it, as tempting as it was. She'd deal with this and then she could wake up tomorrow knowing she'd stuck to her guns.

She swayed a little, and tried grounding herself in place by biting her cheek until it hurt. The only thing she heard coming from outside now was the wind. The ever-present wind and the beginning of rain against the glass. But no tapping—from the branches or anything else.

Slowly, her heartbeat began to go back to a normal rhythm. *See?* she thought. *You're fine. Everything's fine...*

She stood there for another few seconds, just to be sure, and then turned to head for the door.

"Did you have a nice birthday?"

She jumped. There, standing in the doorway, was Eric. As if he'd been conjured up from one of her nightmares. As if he'd found a way to *float* inside without making a sound.

He smiled. "You look surprised. I just stopped by to say hi."

She stared at him, eyes wide. "The door..."

"The door?" He looked innocently behind him. "It was locked, I know. But I picked it."

It was like something out of a movie. But it was too absurd even for that kind of storyline. *He'd picked it?*

"You wouldn't have let me in," he said with a shrug. "So I had to."

She took a step back. And then another. She still had her phone in her hand, open to the text she was going to send to Beau. If only she'd sent it. Eric was watching her like a hawk, there was no way she could call 911 without him stopping her. She thought there was some kind of shortcut for emergency calls, but she had no clue how to do it.

She opened her mouth, wanting to scream at him to get out. Wanting to throw something at him, too, but she couldn't seem to get her body to cooperate. She was frozen. Her limbs dangling from her torso like cooked spaghetti noodles.

"Don't look so terrified, Summer," he said with a smile. Only, it wasn't a friendly smile. It wasn't even a familiar smile. It was something else, and Summer's skin crawled.

"I mean you didn't call me back," he continued. "You didn't write me back. You just cut me out of your life, and we were friends. I mean we still *are* friends. I hope we are, at least. But why didn't you call me back?"

"Call you back..."

"In Eugene?"

She couldn't believe she was standing face to face with him. Having a conversation, even if it was one-sided. He didn't seem to have any idea why she would've wanted to distance herself from him. Or why she might be scared of him now. He had no clue, and that was spine-chilling.

He scratched his head. His mousy-brown hair was stringy. It looked like he hadn't washed it in days. He wore the same black, horn-rimmed glasses that used to be his trademark around the office, only now they didn't seem fun and funky, they looked old and out of style. He had a pair of saggy brown-corduroy pants on and a gray-plaid shirt that was untucked. He'd lost weight since she'd last seen him a few years ago. The shirt hung off his frame as if it were trying to get some purchase but couldn't find any.

"Summer?" he said. His voice had a slight whine to it that set her teeth on edge. "Why didn't you call me back?"

She knew she had to say something but didn't want to say the wrong thing. He was obviously unbalanced and seemed especially unpredictable standing there picking at a button on his shirt now.

"Eric, you need to leave," she said, adding some steel into her voice that she didn't feel. "You're breaking the law."

He grimaced at her. "Oh, I'm breaking the law? Just because I want to see my friend?"

"It's wrong what you're doing. I just want to be left alone."

"Summer…"

He took a step toward her but stopped when she sucked in an audible breath. He knew she was scared of him. She thought he might be enjoying it. It was a sick game. He really was out of his mind.

She gripped her phone behind her back. *Beau...* She wasn't going to be lucky enough that he'd just show up out of nowhere. He didn't even know she was in trouble because she'd never had a chance to text him back.

And then she remembered… She might not be able to call the police without Eric stopping her first—or worse—but the text thread to Beau was open. If she could manage to record a voice memo, all she'd have to do was press Send and try to keep Eric distracted in the meantime. It was a long shot, but she had to try.

She squeezed her phone tighter. There was no way she could do it without looking at the screen, of course. But if she was fast enough…

She clenched her jaw and pulled her phone out. Looking down at the screen, she hit the microphone button.

"Oh," he said. "I can't let you do that."

She took a step backward. Hopefully, it was recording now. All she'd need to do was keep him talking long enough to clue Beau in.

"You need to leave, Eric," she said again. "You broke in, you're trespassing."

"Give me that."

She took another step back and bumped into the workbench behind her. A can of varnish tumbled to the floor and splashed all over the bottom of his pants. The tangy smell burned her nose.

He glanced down, distracted for a precious second, and she pressed Send on the memo with a trembling hand. If Beau got it, he'd call the police. She just had to keep Eric calm until then.

He looked back up at her. "Give it to me," he said quietly.

She waited for as long as she thought she could. Long enough to buy some time.

"Now."

Slowly, she held it out.

He snatched the phone from her hand, glancing at it to presumably make sure the police weren't on the other end of the line, and then tossed it aside. It hit the wall with a resounding thud.

"Why do you have to be like this?" he said through clamped teeth. "You make people think I'm a horrible person, when all I want is to be your friend. That's all I've ever wanted."

"Friends don't act this way."

"How would *you* know how friends act?"

She prayed Beau was calling the police. That he was on his way to her. She couldn't let herself think of what might happen if he wasn't.

"Eric," she said. "Please. Just go, and everything will be okay."

"Sorry, Summer." He stared at her, his gaze filled with anger. "I'm not going anywhere."

Chapter Sixteen

"Come on, Roo. Let's hit it."

Beau watched as the big dog gathered herself on her haunches then jumped into the back seat of his truck.

"She liked that," Mary said, popping another gummy worm into her mouth. Her cheeks bulged with them.

"She did. I wasn't sure about the whole dog park thing, but she did pretty well. Only sent one Chihuahua flying." He was kidding. Kind of. She'd made the poor thing tumble like a potato bug, though.

Mary laughed and climbed into the passenger's seat, her ponytail snatched up by the wind.

Beau looked at the sky. It was almost dark now, but he could make out angry black clouds in the last light of dusk. They were plump with rain. He thought of Summer again, how he hadn't heard from her yet, and frowned. She really must hate him.

He climbed in next to Mary and started the engine. Roo whined from the back seat.

"I know," he said. "You're hungry."

"She's *starving*," Mary said.

Mary was fond of exaggerating lately. You weren't thirsty, you were *parched*—a favorite new word that she'd learned from Frances down the street. You weren't tired, you were *exhausted.* And so on and so forth.

He smiled over at her but he was having trouble getting Summer out of his head. The air around them felt heavy and charged. He was worried about her, thinking about her almost constantly since they'd left the apartment. If she didn't text back pretty soon, he'd call. And if she didn't answer, he'd drive over there. He might not be welcome, but it was a risk he was willing to take.

He looked in the side mirror to check for traffic then pulled out onto the near-empty road.

"Can we get pizza?" Mary asked, twisting around in her seat to scratch Roo's ear.

"Sure. Do you want to call your mom and aunt Poppy, and see if they want to meet us at Mario's?"

"Yeah!"

He leaned to the side and pulled his phone from his back pocket.

"Uncle Beau, you can't check your phone while you're driving," Mary said primly. "It's dangerous."

"You're right, it is. Here. Will you check my texts and make sure I don't have any new ones please?"

Mary grabbed his phone, knowing who he was probably hoping to hear from, and was no doubt happy to assist any way she could.

"There's a voice memo from Summer," she said. "Can I play it?"

Beau looked over. How the hell had he missed that? Talk about a watched pot that never boils.

"Sure," he said, trying not to sound too anxious, which he absolutely was. "Go ahead."

Mary pushed Play and immediately had to turn the

volume on high to hear anything. She held the phone up to her ear, making a strained face.

"It sounds like a butt dial," she said. "Like she was talking to somebody else."

Beau pulled the truck over and put his hazards on. "Here, honey. Let me see."

Mary handed him the phone. The voice memo had been sent just a few minutes ago.

He pushed Play, holding the speaker right next to his ear.

When he heard Summer's voice, the undeniable tremble in it, his stomach turned. His blood went cold with fear for her, with the sickening knowledge that he wasn't there to protect her.

And, beneath it, his fury at that son of a *bitch.* He'd shown up at her house. He'd waited until they'd all started breathing easier and then he'd taken her by surprise.

Clearly, though, Summer wasn't as weak—or as alone—as he'd thought.

Beau stepped on the gas, and the tires squealed on the pavement.

"Uncle Beau?" There was a tinge of fear in Mary's voice.

"Mary, I have to go out to Summer's place. There's someone there who shouldn't be there, and she could be in trouble. I want you to stay in the truck and lock the doors, and keep them locked, no matter what, do you understand?"

He glanced over and she nodded, her blue eyes wide. "Is Summer okay?"

"She's okay," he said. But he didn't feel confident of

that at all. "I need you to call 9-1-1 for me, though, alright? Put them on speaker so I can concentrate on the road."

She did as she was told and when he was done talking to the dispatcher, she hung up and looked over at him. There were tears streaming down her face.

"I'm scared," she said.

Blue lightning zigzagged across the sky, followed by a sharp clap of thunder that reverberated inside the truck's cab. Fat drops of rain began pelting the windshield and Beau had to narrow his eyes to be able to see the road at all. He forced himself to slow down to the speed limit only because Mary was with him.

He reached over and grabbed her hand. "Don't be scared, honey," he said. "It's okay."

"Why would anyone hurt Summer?"

That was a question he couldn't answer. It tore at his heart in a way that terrified him and made him angrier than he'd ever been.

"Can you try calling her?" he asked. "The police are on the way, but we'll probably get there before they do. We're only a few minutes away now. Maybe she'll answer." He prayed she would.

Mary put the phone on speaker and dialed Summer's number. It rang once, twice, three times. And then went to voicemail with a finality that Beau wasn't prepared for. His throat tightened, his chest compressing to the point that it was hard to take a full breath. If anything happened to her… It was a thought he hadn't allowed himself to explore until just now. It was that dark thing that went along with loving someone, with needing them. If you opened yourself up to those things, you opened yourself up to the possibility of getting swallowed whole by that darkness, and that felt incomprehensible. Yet there he was. Loving her. Scared of losing her. As much as he'd tried to push it away this whole time, it had happened anyway. And wasn't that how life was supposed to be? It happened to you. The good things. And the bad.

Roo whined from the back. She was afraid of thunder. She was always reduced to a huge, hairy puddle during storms, and he usually put her in the bathroom with the fan going during the worst ones.

"I'm sorry, girl," he said, his voice low. He gripped the wheel in his fists, his thoughts going a hundred miles an hour.

Beside him, Mary sniffled softly.

Ahead, he could see the lights of Summer's place. The porch lights and the light to the shop, which he knew would usually be dark by now. His shoulders and back tightened in anticipation. He strained to see through the torrents of rain streaming down the windshield. Hoping to catch a glimpse of Summer in the window, safe in her little house.

But as they got closer, the feeling of dread only intensified. He turned onto her driveway and they bounced over the potholes in the road. Mary gripped the door handle with one hand and put her other hand on Roo to comfort her.

"You stay in the truck, do you hear me?" he said. He practically barked it, beyond sugarcoating anything at this point. He could see the door to the shop was open, a man standing inside. His jaw clenched. If this guy touched one hair on her head…

"What if the police don't come?" Mary asked.

"They'll be here any minute."

"But what are you going to do? What if he hurts you?"

"He won't. It'll be okay. But you stay in the truck." He slammed his foot on the brake, bringing the truck to a jolting stop in front of the shop. He turned to look at his niece as he yanked his seat belt off. "Promise me, Mary. Do *not* open this door."

She looked terrified. "I promise."

He had no idea what this guy was capable of. If he'd already done something beyond comprehending…

Roo growled from the back seat, pricking her ears toward the shop, as if she could read his mind. There was no doubt she sensed his stress and he patted her quickly as he opened the door into the wind and rain.

"Stay," he said. More to Mary than to Roo.

He jogged toward the shop, shielding his eyes from the stinging rain. "Summer!"

There was a loud crash from inside. A thud of some kind. And then her voice. "Beau!"

He barreled through the half-open door, nearly running into the man standing in the middle of the room. He barely had time to register Summer on the ground, crumpled next to the wall as if she'd been thrown there. And then Eric came at him. He was holding something in his hand, something that glinted in the light. Thunder crashed overhead, shaking the windows. Rattling Beau's teeth inside his head.

He watched the man run toward him like he was moving in slow motion. He wore a crazed look on his face. His glasses were hanging off one ear and he was yelling something incoherent. Beau planted his feet on the ground, bracing himself.

And then Eric made contact, raising what he held in his hand. A knife. It finally registered in Beau's brain—dots that hadn't wanted to be connected a few seconds before were now in a neat row.

Summer screamed.

Beau could've ducked. He could've kicked the guy, or pushed him, or done any number of things. But he'd always thrown a good punch. It was the same reason that his fishing line had sailed impossibly far through the air during those championship tournaments. Effortless. That's how they used to describe his cast on ESPN. He had a strong arm. Maybe it wasn't as strong as it used to be, it was still healing, but it could still get the job done. He knew this in his heart as he drew back, squeezed his hand into a fist and let it fly.

He made contact with Eric's face with a sickening *smack*! The guy's glasses flew off and he stumbled backward. Blood gushed from his nose.

There was a scorching pain in Beau's shoulder. Stars exploded behind his eyes. He'd known he'd only have that one punch. But it had been a good one. He prayed it would be enough, that Eric would fall from the force of the blow, that he would drop the knife in his hand.

Summer scrambled to her feet.

"Run!" Beau shouted at her.

She looked frantically around. Probably trying to find something she could use as a weapon.

Eric stood there for a second, stunned. Holding his cheek in one hand and the knife in the other.

"*Now*, Summer!"

She darted past, but Eric lunged at her, quicker.

"I just want to be your friend!" he cried. "Why can't you understand that? *Why?*"

He grabbed the hem of her shirt and yanked, pulling her toward him. He still had the knife in his hand, the ugly blade flashing along with the lighting outside. For a second, the room flickered in blue. And then thunder crashed.

Beau grabbed for the other man, the pain in his shoulder coursing down his arm and up his neck like a hot poker. But adrenaline was a wonderful thing and he was able to help Summer wrestle out of his grip.

"Go!"

She ran for the door, leaving Eric to turn on him with his full rage.

There was a blur of gray in Beau's peripheral vision and he whipped around in time to see Roo launch herself into the air. For a second, he couldn't comprehend what was happening, it was all so fast, so chaotic. But when the dog hit Eric's chest, he fell to the ground like a sack of potatoes.

The knife clattered to the floor, and Roo yelped as he shoved her viciously. But then she growled and bit down on his arm, hard. Police cars tore down the driveway, sirens wailing—music to Beau's ears.

Leaning down, he hauled the dog off Eric. And with the last of the strength in his shoulder, he carried her outside where the police were skidding to a stop in front of the shop.

Eric stumbled out after him, his hands raised in the air. The red and blue lights from the two cruisers flashed across his face as thunder rumbled overhead and rain soaked his shirt.

"I just want to be her friend," he said.

Beau set Roo gently down in the rain, where she immediately favored her front leg. Holding her collar, he watched as Ben Martinez carefully approached the other man and then handcuffed him. He had no fight left, just looked sad and confused by what he'd done.

Summer and Mary ran over to Beau, the girl throwing her arms around Roo with a sob.

"Is she going to be okay?" she asked, her tears indistinguishable from the rain.

Beau frowned down at the dog. She'd been protecting him. Mary had let her out and she'd come to his aid. She was a loyal friend. A good dog to her core.

"She's going to be fine, honey. It's just her leg. She's going to be okay."

"Ma'am?"

They turned to see a young female officer standing there in the pouring rain. Her face was drawn, serious. She wore a black rain jacket that had the police emblem on the chest, but the hood had blown off in the wind. Her short hair was dripping, her skin soaked.

"Can you tell me what happened here tonight?"

"I'm so glad you're here," Summer said. "Can we go inside where it's dry?"

"Of course."

Summer stood on her tiptoes and gave Beau a quick kiss on the cheek. Her lips were warm and sweet, a promise of forgiveness. Maybe something more. Time would tell.

And then she was heading into her house, with the officer and Mary following close behind. Steady light spilled from the old windows, a comforting beacon in the storm.

Beau tugged lightly on Roo's collar, and she began limping gingerly next to him. Which was a good thing—he wouldn't have been able to pick her up again. His shoulder wouldn't have it. The adrenaline had eased and the pain had come like a tidal wave. He felt queasy with it.

He could hear Chief Martinez reading Eric his rights behind him. Beau had no idea what would've happened if he'd gotten there any later than he had. If Roo hadn't tackled Eric to the ground when she had. If the police hadn't come when they had… All questions he'd have to process later, when his heartbeat had slowed and the shock had worn off. He could've lost Summer tonight. The thought was too much to bear.

He understood then, even if it hadn't completely sunk in yet, that he would be changed by this. That things from this point on would be different.

As they should be.

Summer sat in Dr. Poet's waiting room, her hair a mass of damp curls on the back of her neck. Beau was sitting on her left—Mary, Cora and Poppy on her right. Dr. Poet and his wife, Rebecca, had opened his office for them and said they were all welcome to stay while he took X-rays and casted Roo's broken leg. And stay they had. They'd made themselves as comfortable as possible on the hard plastic chairs, and Cora had just brought coffee, and hot chocolate for Mary.

Summer looked over at Beau who was leaning back in his chair, staring into space. He'd been quiet since the police had questioned them, since they'd driven Eric away. He would presumably be locked up for a while, and that was a good thing. But everything else about this night had her turned inside out. She knew Eric was responsible for what had happened, and nobody else, but she couldn't help feeling like it was her fault anyway. If she and Beau hadn't reconnected...

There was just no analyzing it, no way of breaking it down, that made it any easier to understand. It was what it was, and she was going to have to move forward—away from being the victim of a stalker. Counseling would help with the trauma, leaning on her friends and family for support. She was lucky to have resources and people who cared about her. She just wondered how the rest of her life was going to look.

She reached over and took Beau's hand. He looked down at their linked fingers and smiled. Cora and Poppy were quietly playing a game with Mary on her phone, and the room felt peaceful with the storm having blown itself out. She lay her head on Beau's shoulder, careful not to jostle him any. Cora had also brought some leftover pain medication from his surgery, but he'd be going to the hospital after this, and she was afraid of what they'd say. They'd order X-rays, probably an ultrasound. And then they'd figure out how he'd be able to move forward, too. Would he ever be able to fish again? Only time would tell.

She wondered what he was thinking as she breathed in his familiar spicy scent. If he was blaming her in any way. All she knew for sure was that she was more in love with him now than ever. He'd come to her when she'd needed him most. He'd put himself in harm's way for her. And he was holding her hand now, rubbing his thumb gently across her knuckles in a way that filled her up. She didn't know what the future looked like for her and Beau, tonight might be all they had left. But she was going to soak up every minute of it while she could and would worry about the rest later.

Beau shifted next to her and she raised her head. "Sorry. Does that hurt?"

He wiggled his fingers, but when she tried taking her hand away, he reached out and grabbed it. "It hurts, but it's not life or death. I'll be fine."

She nodded, watching him. He'd always been hard to read, but right now it was almost impossible. She could see the emotion clearly etched across his face, though. She tried to prepare herself for the worst but, honestly, how much worse could it get? He'd already decided to leave. Really, she had nothing to lose.

The muscles in his jaw bunched as he continued staring down at their hands, linked, intertwined. She could see the pulse in his neck, where his skin was so tanned and his hair fell past his ears. He'd let it grow since moving to Christmas Bay. It was impossibly sexy, sun-bleached, and making her want to run her hands through it.

He looked at her with those ocean-blue eyes and there was an expression in them that made her catch her breath. They were so intent, so focused, that it felt like he could see right into her. She thought her feelings should probably be pretty obvious by now, even without those X-ray eyes. The love she had for Beau was almost palpable.

"I'm sorry," he said, his voice gravelly.

"Sorry…for what?"

He licked his lips. Paused. Then took a visible breath. "For all of it. For not giving us a chance. Again."

It wasn't the words that caught her off guard. He'd said this kind of thing before and she understood why. He did care for her, but he cared about fishing more. At least, that's what she used to think. But now, as she waited for what he was going to say next, there was a feeling that it would be meaningful. If his tone, if the look in his eyes, meant anything at all.

"I don't know why I've been so hesitant to let anyone in," he continued. "I don't know why I never let you in. When it counted. That when you trusted me most, I let you down."

She squeezed his hand. Felt the calluses on his fingers scrape against her skin. There was something erotic about that. She remembered what it felt like to have him touch her naked body. How she *had* trusted him once, with every fiber of her being, and he'd still broken her heart.

"But you didn't let me down," she said and knew that was true. There were more ways to trust someone than just with your heart. "You came tonight. I'll never forget that. We don't have to be together for me to love you. Maybe that's what I've been wanting all along. Permission to love you, no matter what."

He smiled. Then looked past her to Mary, Cora and Poppy, who were conspicuously quiet now, the game on Mary's phone long forgotten.

"Uh," Poppy said. "Sorry. We were trying not to listen."

"Speak for yourself," Mary said.

Summer laughed. It was impossible not to. It was a moment of levity that they all needed. The heaviness in the room had been almost too much to bear.

Beau nudged her in the side. "Want to go outside for a few minutes? Get some fresh air? The stars are finally out, it's turning into a pretty night."

"I'd love that."

They stood, Beau tucking his arm close to his side. He was only a few weeks out from his surgery. She was no doctor, but she knew that reinjuring it now would almost certainly be catastrophic for the joint.

She tried not to think about that as he opened the door for her with his other hand and she walked past him into the damp summer night. The pavement in the small parking lot glistened black from the rain. The air felt cool on Summer's skin, smelling heavenly and clean. She looked up at the sky and Beau had been right—the stars were out in force. They sparkled brilliantly against the velvety backdrop of space. It made her feel small and insignificant. But at the same time it gave her an intense appreciation to be alive and well. Things could've been different tonight. As bad as they'd ended, they could've gone much worse.

She contemplated that as she wrapped her arms around herself, continuing to look up at the sky in wonder.

"There are so many," she said.

He looked up, too. But then shifted his gaze to her.

"What?" she asked.

"You."

"What about me?"

"You're beautiful."

"I'm not."

"You know you are."

She smiled.

"Look at me," he said.

Slowly, she turned until she was facing him. He was so handsome under the moonlight, so familiar. He was her first love. Her only love. A hard thing to admit when things had ended so badly between them, at least the first time. But it was what it was.

"If you hadn't come when you did," she said, "I don't know what would've happened. Thank you for that."

"There's no need to thank me, Summer."

"There is," she said. "Your shoulder…"

He paused, looking up at the stars. Seeming to take them in. Seeming to be searching for something.

In her heart, she felt like they were on the cusp of something, but she didn't know what. Her pulse skipped, reminding her that no matter what happened between her and Beau, she would survive it. Just like she'd survived before. But she didn't want Beau to be something she had to survive. She didn't want him to be someone she remembered years from now and wondered *What if?* As she waited for him to continue, she braced herself, like she had so many times before, and reminded herself to stay in the moment. Just enjoy what they had right now, under these incredible stars.

"I think…" His gaze found hers again, his eyes dark and brooding. "I think I'm done with sportfishing."

She stared up at him. She wanted so many things right then but she was afraid to want them, too. Because wanting was very close to needing. Sometimes those two things felt indistinguishable. At least, when it came to Beau.

"I'm sorry…what?"

The corners of his mouth tilted a little. "Hard to believe, huh?"

"I'm just not sure I heard you right."

He reached up and cupped her face in his good hand, keeping his other arm very still. He rubbed his thumb across her cheekbone and she felt herself leaning toward him like a magnet. He had that kind of pull over her.

"You heard me right," he said.

"Why would you be done? It's what you love."

"You're right. I do love it. But since coming back to Christmas Bay, I've learned there are things that I love more."

Her entire body trembled as she waited for him to go on. It was like she'd been waiting forever, and she felt strange, like she was watching this happen to someone else. Some other woman, in some other lifetime.

"My family is here," he said. "My grandfather's shop, which is part of our history, and his entire legacy. Mary's here, and she really needs a father figure right now…" He paused, his gaze dropping momentarily to her mouth. "And you're here."

"I don't want to be the reason you give up fishing, Beau," Summer said quietly. "Where would that leave us?"

"Happy," he said.

She shook her head. It was everything she'd wanted since college, everything she'd wanted since he'd come back to Christmas Bay. But she'd been trying so hard to convince herself that she didn't want him anymore, that she was afraid to believe him. Even now.

"Is this because of your shoulder?" she asked. "Because of what you think the X-rays might say?"

"I don't care what they say."

"But—"

He shook his head. "This doesn't have anything to do with my shoulder."

She wondered how that could possibly be. But the expression on his face said he needed her to hear him out. So she hugged herself in the damp night air, breathing in the scent of rain, and stayed quiet, opening herself up to what he had to say.

"I think I'd made my mind up the second you walked out of the shop the other day," he said. "The day I lost my sponsorship. It took me a while to accept it for what it was, but seeing you go… I think I started changing. Figuring out what I wanted and what I didn't want. And I didn't want to see you go. Not having you felt worse than not having my career anymore. And that's when I knew."

Her heart squeezed. "You can fish and have me, too, Beau. You don't have to choose."

Smiling at that, he tucked her hair behind her ear. So tenderly that she thought she might break wide open right then and there. She'd never felt more vulnerable, more at another person's mercy in her life. It was a scary feeling. It was a humbling feeling.

"The thing is," he said. "I don't want to be split, part of me one place and the other part somewhere else. I'm tired of not belonging anywhere, or feeling like I don't have a home. I've been afraid to admit it, even to myself, but I think I needed this…this grounding, for a long time. I think my grandpa knew that, and that's why he asked us to do this. He knew we all needed to come back here for different reasons. And my reason was that

I was flailing. I was missing a piece of me. And now I've found it again."

He leaned down to kiss her on the cheek. A soft, sweet, gentle kiss, but it rocked her where she stood.

"I've found you again," he said.

"Beau..."

"I understand if you need to think about it. I don't know what this looks like from here on out. I haven't exactly had many long-term relationships in my life, but I can't think of anyone I want to give it a shot with more. If you can trust me. If you can love me again."

Summer's eyes blurred. She slipped her arms around his trim waist and lay her head against his chest. "I've never stopped loving you, Beau."

He kissed the top of her head. She felt his heart beating against her cheek, strong and sure, and she didn't think she'd ever felt safer in her life. There were no promises, no guarantees, especially with love. But this was the most she could ask for. The promise of a new beginning.

He wrapped his good arm around her, burying his hand in her hair. She pulled away enough to look up at him and he leaned down and kissed her. His lips tasted like home. He felt like home. She understood what he meant by being grounded here; she was grounded here, too. And maybe they grounded each other. She thought it was a nice way of looking at it as his mouth moved over hers. As she felt goose bumps pop up on her skin. As the stars twinkled overhead and the ocean waves crashed in the distance.

She felt like she'd been given another chance. Life in a small town doing what she loved—tinkering with old furniture and making it glow again. She'd watched the patina rub off, the luster underneath becoming brighter and brighter, and now here she was. On the verge of something special, of something beautiful. Would it last? The only way to know for sure was to jump in feet first, just like she'd done in that fishing hole all those weeks ago. She'd jump right in and wait for him to follow.

The water was perfect.

Epilogue

Beau shifted on the bed. He had cabin fever—and that was putting it mildly. He was also sick of having to stay in one position like this, but his shoulder required rest and, if he had any hopes of being able to use it again with most of his range of motion, and also without near constant pain and stiffness in the future, he needed to follow his doctor's orders.

His sportfishing career was definitely over. That was a given. When he'd heard the news, he hadn't been surprised. And it also hadn't knocked the wind out of him like he'd expected it to. It was a loss, but a loss he could live with. And he'd found peace with it. A gentle peace that brought good memories of a well-loved career that had run its course. What more could he ask for?

These days, Beau was all about counting his blessings. There were several of them, but at the top of the list was Summer. Her now-incarcerated stalker had admitted to police that he'd come to her house prepared to hurt her that night. She'd been lucky. They'd all been lucky. It was the kind of life-changing moment that made you take stock of what you had. And how you wanted to live from that point on.

He shifted again, trying to get comfortable, and lay his hand on Roo's side. She was stretched out beside him, her body almost as long as his on the bed. She couldn't jump up there by herself at the moment because of her bright pink cast, but Beau had gotten her a ramp and had shown her how to walk up and down it. She'd been scared of it at first, but she was a champ and had forged ahead anyway.

She was their hero. She'd even been featured on the news and in a local newspaper article that had gone viral. She was a Christmas Bay celebrity. But most of all, she'd been Beau's constant and most faithful friend in the days after his surgery.

Well, she and Summer.

Beau looked up at the clock now. She'd be here any minute. His things were neatly stacked in a few boxes in the corner, all packed up and ready to go. The rest of his stuff was in storage, where it would stay until he was moved into his new place. But there was no hurry. For the first time in his life, he was content to take things as they came. And most of all, not to sweat the small stuff. He'd decided to go back to college to finish his bachelor's and eventually get his MBA, and was finding that not sweating the small stuff was an absolute necessity if he wasn't going to drive himself crazy with the details. It would all fall into place. He'd move into his rental by the beach, help his cousins in the shop, and go to school to learn how to really grow their business. Maybe even expand it. It would all work out the way it was supposed to. In due time.

But one thing he still wasn't very good at was patience. At least, where Summer was concerned. He'd asked her to move in with him a few days ago and she hadn't given him an answer yet. He kept telling himself it was a good thing that she was taking her time to think about it. He understood her hesitation, her wanting to make sure it was the right decision. After all, it might feel pretty fast. He was sure it *looked* fast to their family and friends. To Beau, it was the only thing he wanted. To start building a relationship, a life, with the woman he loved. And, yeah. It might seem like they were putting the cart before the horse, but so be it. He was leading with his heart for once. And that felt good.

He heard his cousins talking and laughing from the living room. Poppy had given up her bedroom for his recovery, but lately, recovery or not, he found himself wanting to be where they were. Where the laughter was. Where the love was.

Pushing himself up with his good arm, he looked over at the closed door, hearing another voice mingled with theirs. His heart, as it so often did now, thumped at the sound. At the anticipation of seeing her. He felt like the clock had been turned back to when he was younger and less jaded about life. He was excited to see his girlfriend. And did it get any better than that? For Beau, he wasn't sure it did. At least, that's how it felt. Good. Happy. *Right*.

The door opened a crack and she peeked her head in. Her fiery hair was a cascade of waves falling past her pretty face. Her freckles popped. She'd been working outside in the sun and it showed. She had a healthy glow. She looked happy. But he knew it was still hard for her to trust this. Once bitten, twice shy.

Even so, they'd fallen into a groove that was so natural sometimes it felt like they'd been together their entire lives. That was a good feeling. He'd come back home again. He'd found love. He'd found his place in this small part of the world.

She smiled. "I thought you might be sleeping."

Roo raised her head and thumped her tail against Beau's thigh.

"I'm tired of sleeping. I've been looking forward to seeing you."

"I brought you something."

"If it's what I think it is, I might have to ask you to marry me."

Color filled her cheeks as she stepped inside. She was wearing an emerald-green dress that matched her eyes. She was a vision.

"If I'd known that cookies were the way to your heart, I would've been baking the entire time."

She walked over and set a Tupperware container next to his bed. He could see the cookies inside—big, fat, chocolate-chip cookies that looked melty and warm. Their sugary scent filled the room and his stomach growled.

She sat on the edge of his bed and Roo licked her hand. She scratched the dog behind the ears before leaning down to give Beau a long, lingering kiss.

"How are you feeling?" she asked when she pulled away.

"Better, now that you're here. Thank you for the cookies."

"You're welcome."

"I'm ready to be out of this bed."

"Have you tried the recliner?"

"That's tomorrow's adventure. I'm trying to stick to the doctor's timeline."

"I'm proud of you."

"Yeah, well…" He reached up and rubbed her back. "I'm trying."

She watched him, her gaze dropping to his mouth. He could smell her perfume, light and fresh, reminding him of the day they'd jumped into the fishing hole and shared that kiss. The one that had reignited the fire between them. Or that's how Beau had thought of it at the time. Now he knew that fire had never gone out. It had been burning underneath the surface the entire time.

"What are you thinking?" he asked.

Her gaze found his and he could see she was hesitant to say.

Frowning, he sat up straighter. "What is it, baby?"

"I've been thinking about moving in together…"

His heart beat just a little slower at her hesitation. It was possible she was about to tell him that she'd made up her mind, that it wasn't a good idea. And that would gut him. But as he sat there waiting for her to finish, he knew he'd wait for her. Maybe living together felt too nontraditional for her, and then he might have to ask her to marry him. For real this time. Cookies be damned.

"I'd have to rent my house out," she said slowly. "I'd have to lease a shop to work in."

He'd known these things could be deal breakers for her. They were big issues; things that she might not want to do now, or ever. Still, he'd hoped…

"And Tank," she said. "He'd have to be boarded somewhere, and I wouldn't get to see him as often as if he were just right outside my house."

He squeezed her hand. "I know," he said. "I get it."

"I want you to know I thought about it, Beau. I really did."

"You don't have to explain. I kind of sprung this on you. It was fast." He smiled. "I blame the cookies."

"Magic cookies."

"I guess. But I would've fallen in love with you anyway. With or without them."

"That's good to know. In case I ever lose the touch."

He reached up and cupped her face in his hand, rubbing his thumb over her cheekbone. "I'm glad you're here."

"I'm sorry about not moving into your place."

"It's okay."

"So what about you moving into mine?"

He stared at her. "What…?"

She smiled, her eyes twinkling. "What if you moved in with me? To my house? I know you put a deposit down on your rental, but I bet you could get it back. And I think you'd love it out there—the fresh air, the view…" She paused and leaned close to kiss him again. This time there was an urgency in her lips and excitement that he could feel. She wanted this. She wanted him to want it, too.

"And the best part," she finished softly, "is that there's a creek on my neighbor's property that branches off from the river. There's a little fishing hole there with your name on it. I've already asked, and he said you can fish there any time you want. He said he'd be honored to have *the* Beau Evers fishing on his land. He's a fan."

Beau laughed. “No more sponsors, but there are still perks.”

“What do you say?” She chewed the inside of her cheek, her lips forming a perfect kissable heart. It looked like she was worried that he’d say no, that he might be too invested in his own plans, his own way of doing things. After all, that’s how it had been almost a decade ago when he’d broken things off with her on that autumn day. He wasn’t sure how he’d ever walked away from Summer, but he had. And she was looking at him now like she remembered it very well. It was a moment tattooed on her heart.

What she didn’t know was that it was tattooed on his, too. All of it. The pain and regret and sadness from leaving her was something he’d never forget. And it was that visceral memory that had shaped him into the man he was today. Loss did things to you. The loss of Summer, the loss of his grandfather, the loss of his career. But loss also made room for possibility, too. And that was what was growing inside him now. The possibility of a brand-new life. It didn’t matter where he set down roots, just as long as he set them down with the people he loved.

He took her hand and rubbed his thumb across her knuckles. He’d learned that sometimes the simplest things made him the happiest. Like sitting there holding her hand.

“Beau?”

He looked at her. He was in love. He was home. He had his whole life ahead of him, if he was lucky. Did it get any better than that?

“Sorry,” he said. “I was just thinking.”

“About?”

"About how you caught me."

She smiled. "Just like a fish."

"Exactly," he said, leaning in for another kiss. He couldn't get enough of her kisses. "Hook, line, and sinker."

* * * * *

Don't miss Cora's story,
the next installment in Hearts on Main Street
Kaylie Newell's new miniseries for
Harlequin Special Edition
Coming soon!

And catch up with Poppy's story
Flirting With the Past
Available now, wherever Harlequin books
and ebooks are sold!